THE OREGON STORY

A NOVEL BY
DEVIK SCHREINER

The Oregon Story

Published by:

Robertson Publishing™
www.RobertsonPublishing.com

Devik Schreiner has also written:
"Search A Darker Sky, A Cleft Mind"

Acknowledgements

Writing a book is like putting together a puzzle, except I don't really know what I am making until it begins to take shape, and even then, when it's finished, it's quite different than what I thought it was going to be. The following people each provided a piece of the puzzle, for which I am very grateful.

- Emmanuela Raquelle, whose suggestions for word flow, consistency and simplification made the book better.

- Annie Andreeva, whose Oxford-trained eye for errors helped keep my story straight.

- Eagle-Eye Bird.

- Jeanne Yee, for her patience and vision as an artist and karmic balancer.

- Dr. Jonathan Miller, Chair of the Department of Geology at San Jose State University, for his time in sharing the physical characteristics of lava tubes.

- Seven Towns Ltd., for granting me permission to use the description of the Rubik's Cube in the book.

- Miyako Singer at Counterpoint, LLC/Soft Skull Press for allowing me to use Wendell Berry's amazing poem.

- Lucas, Emi, Samika, Olive, Maya, Wesley, Claryssa, Tanay, Lexi, Laya, Nikhil, Yoav, Skye, Liv, Pixie, Mateen, Nathan, Sofia, Lindsay, Andrew, Zoe, Nolan, Beaver(!), Will, Alex Squared, Carina, Sander, Dylan, and Miles.

- Elzene Yancey, whose appreciation for life, love of learning, and excitement about my teaching and writing careers motivates me.

"To Know the Dark"

To go in the dark with a light is to know the light.
To know the dark, go dark. Go without the sight,
and find that the dark, too, blooms and sings,
and is traveled by dark feet and dark wings.

Wendell Berry

THE OREGON STORY

Chapter I: The Bag Below the Sidewalk

You did it.

You found the cube.

It's a regular Rubik's Cube. Plastic. Eight corner pieces. Twelve middle edges. Six center squares. Maybe you've solved one, or tried to.

But the cube is only a storage vessel. It holds a material that you have come to know as C-Metal. Some of what you've heard about this material is true. Much isn't. But for now, we need to be clear on some important rules:

1. Don't lose the cube. Either keep it with you or in a place no one knows about.

2. Only handle the cube when necessary. Don't turn the cube, and don't take it apart. C-Metal isn't dangerous; you just need to be ready to handle it, and right now, you're not. Not yet.

3. I know this will sound strange, but try not to think about the cube too much. In time, you'll become more familiar with the material inside of it, and you will understand.

As I write this, it's your third grade year at Benjamin Harrison Elementary School. Your sister, Alyssa, is four years old. I work at Arch-Tech, a small architectural firm in downtown Bent Valley. I'm at Skippy's, a coffee shop a few blocks from work. I like the privacy. I meet one of my co-workers, Sebastian, here. He's one of the few people at Arch-Tech that I trust.

Justin, I know you have questions. I can't answer them right now. So instead, I am going to tell you a story. It's about something that happened to me when I was your age, something that changed my life, and will change your life, too.

Chapter II: The Slip

My mother and I lived deep in the hills of eastern Oregon, and I was going to be alone, really alone, for the first time in my life. She was taking our beat-up old four-wheel drive truck to town, entrusting me with the property for at least a day, maybe two. Maybe more. With the wet weather and treacherous road conditions, it was impossible to nail down exactly when she would return. But I wasn't worried. I could handle it.

I was at the woodpile when I heard our truck's big tires kicking up gravel. I looked up to see it moving slowly down the muddy road. Then, right before the truck disappeared behind the bend, my mom leaned out the window and looked back at me. "Bring in extra firewood," she called out. "It's supposed to get cold." All these years later, I still hear those words, crystal clear.

One last piece. I lifted the splitting maul above my head and paused, ready to strike. I put a little something extra into it and split it right down the middle, and then left the maul leaning against the woodpile. The last few days, I had split enough pine, oak, and madrone to keep the fire going for at least a few weeks, if not longer. And that wasn't even counting the two cords of wood I had already stacked. One finger at a time, I pulled the grimy leather gloves off my hands, letting them fall to the ground.

Chopping firewood was hard work, especially for a skinny 12-year-old, but I took pride in it. Just two years back, I could barely lift the axe; but after my growth spurt, my mom depended on me for a supply of wood to keep her and me warm during the wet winter months.

My dad was an axe man; he felled trees for a living. I have faint memories of him coming home after being gone for days,

3

smelling like birch and cedar, oak and spruce, standing in the mudroom, shaking the sawdust off his clothes. He never said much to me. Sometimes he yelled at my mom. He never stayed long. And then one day he was gone, and he didn't come back.

I grew up alone, but not lonely. Because properties were so spread out up in the mountains, I didn't have many friends around. Sometimes, neighbors would come down and visit from their places, miles away, or we would go to them. Not often, though. It made socializing tough. Most kids grow up with other kids around, to talk to and play with and get to know. I didn't have that. It was just me and my mom.

I spent a lot of my time outside, making up games, building forts, exploring. But because of the Oregon weather, there were many days when it wasn't possible to be outside. And we didn't have TV. There were no cell phones or texting, no Internet or gaming systems, no social networking.

So I read. History. Science. Science fiction. Maybe that sounds boring to you. Not to me. Science fiction was my favorite. Most of my mom's sci-fi collection was from the 40s, 50s and 60s, stories about aliens and space travel and incredibly futuristic technology. What I liked most about science fiction was that no matter where the books' characters were from, or what year it was, they thought and felt the same way you or I or anyone might think or feel. There could be some freaky creature on a planet in a distant galaxy, but he or she (or it) still felt the same things that people feel here on Earth. I could always relate to the characters. I guess without friends you make do.

Oregon winters aren't as bad as people think, my mom used to say - they're worse. It was always either about to rain, raining, or had just finished raining. The soil beneath my feet bubbled up around my muddy boots as I bent down and wrapped my arms around three pieces of pine. They were older, dry pieces that would be perfect for the evening fire. I knew right away that I should have only picked up two. My mistake was not letting a piece fall to the ground and making an extra trip. Instead, holding one of the pieces awkwardly between my left arm and my ribs, I stood up and began the treacherous walk up the mucky trail that led to the house.

A month before, in anticipation of the inevitable torrent of water that would run down from the highland, through our property and into Black Creek, I had dug steps into the trail. As I struggled with the wood, I lost my balance and began to fall. But instead of emptying my arms and trying to catch myself, I kept hold of the wood and tried to regain my balance.

I failed. Time slowed down. I knew that I was going to be hurt, but there was nothing I could do about it. I fell.

And then, nothing.

Chapter III: An Unexpected Visitor

The first thing I was aware of was heat; a familiar, pulsing warmth. Even with my eyes closed, I knew it was from the fire burning in the hearth in the corner of our small living room. I opened my eyes a sliver, enough to follow the shadows that flickered and danced on the ceiling. It was dark out.

I was almost able to get up on a knee, but a wave of dizziness coursed through me and I fell back down. My right side hurt badly. I felt my face; it was swollen from the fall and caked with dry, crusty mud. *Could have been worse*, I thought. *My mom's home early from town, and she pulled me up to the house after I fell. Wait, home early? She just left. That doesn't make sense.*

"Mom." There was no response. I called out louder:

"Mom."

"Your mom's not here."

The voice was deep and cold and totally unfamiliar. Chills raced through me. My mind hurtled through the possibilities, trying to find an explanation:

Maybe my mom had turned around because she had forgotten something. After discovering me at the woodpile, she went to get help, and brought back this guy. Except she would never have left me alone here, injured. She would have stayed here with me or taken me with her.

Or maybe he's a neighbor who was on a hike and noticed me and pulled me up to the house. Except none of the neighbors would walk through our property without permission. And I knew our neighbors. I didn't know that voice.

There was only one real possibility. The man had come to rob us, discovered me by the woodpile, and carried me into the house. He could have hurt me, but he hadn't. Not yet. He wanted something, something in the house, and was waiting for me to wake up so he could make me tell him where it was. Except I had no idea what it was.

The floorboards creaked in the kitchen. Heavy footsteps moved toward me. My mom had once told me about a hunter who was approached by a black bear. The hunter immediately played dead. The bear had sniffed around the terrified man, even turning him over with his huge snout. Then, deciding there was nothing of interest, the bear wandered off. I didn't know what else to do. As the man got close to me, I moaned, turned my head to the side, and pretended to lose consciousness.

The footsteps stopped. I heard the pops and snaps of air pockets in the firewood exploding in the hearth. I tried to breathe like someone who was unconscious would breathe.

I could hear my mom's voice in my head: "Danny, living up here, away from everything and everybody, can be dangerous. A day may come when you'll have to face a challenge. I don't know what the challenge will be, but to conquer it, you'll need to rely on everything you've learned living up here in the woods. I only pray I'm here to help you when that happens." *That day is here,* I thought. *And you're not.*

The footsteps faded away. I needed to get a look at the man. I opened an eye and looked toward the kitchen. I heard the refrigerator close and the man walked over to the sink, his back to me.

He was very tall and built like a truck. He had on dirty denim overalls with a stained white tank top underneath. His thick

7

arms were covered by dark and blurry tattoos. The stranger had long, black hair that hung down to his shoulders. He had on muddy, unlaced work boots. I couldn't see his face.

Chapter IV: Jump, Drop, and Roll

I had to get out. I needed the red emergency bag in my mom's bedroom. The bag held supplies that would be critical if I was to be on my own in the woods. I would take the bag from under the bed, and a jacket, and escape out the back window. From there, I'd move to the south side of the house, out behind the woodpile, to the utility shed. I would cut one of the cables connecting the solar panels to the batteries that delivered power to the house. That way, I could give myself an extra minute's head start in case the man went after me. I'd have the advantage of knowing the surrounding area well, even in the dark. It was now or never.

When I got to my hands and knees, I knew I was hurt. It felt as though someone had used my ribs as a punching bag. Staying low and silent, I crawled into the bedroom.

I froze. I thought I heard the water running, but I wasn't sure. Stretching my arm out under the bed I wrapped my fingers around a strap and grabbed it and pulled. It was heavier than I remembered. That was good. I crawled over to the window and sat below it, my back to the wall, trying to catch my breath.

The chance of the window opening on the first try I put at 50/50. The unstable land mass on which the house was built shifted often, jamming shut doors and windows. Some nights the house sounded like it was alive: eerie creaks and groans from below. It wasn't scary; I was used to it. But sometimes, the next morning, it took a crowbar to loosen up a window or to unjam a door. That night I needed the window to open on the first try.

I wrapped the strap of the bag around my wrist, got on my knees, braced myself, and pushed up on the window as hard as I could. My ribs hurt so badly that I wanted to scream.

It wouldn't budge. I looked around the room and noticed the wooden chair tucked under my mom's desk. I dropped low again and moved around the bed, grabbed one of the chair legs, and inched back to my position below the window.

The water in the sink cascaded off of plates and glasses. He was doing the dishes! Why? It made no sense. The water stopped and there were footsteps again. Visible in the closet was my warmest coat, a waterproof goose-down winter jacket. I needed it, but I couldn't be caught on the wrong side of the bed. I had to leave the jacket.

It was time. I grabbed the two back legs of the chair. Then, in one fluid motion, I stood up, closed my eyes, and smashed the chair through the double-pane bedroom window.

"Hey, what the - "

Shielding my face with the bag, I launched shoulder-first through the window, praying that the jagged shards of glass wouldn't shred any veins. I tucked my body into a ball as glass exploded around me. My left shoulder hit the ground first and I rolled forward.

It was raining. The man was screaming, unintelligible words ripping through the cold air, muffled by the wind and raindrops. I didn't know if the glass had cut me; the adrenaline coursing through me was masking the pain of any injuries I might have received. I jumped up and ran around to the other side of the house and raced down the same muddy steps that I had fallen on earlier that day.

I was counting on the man expecting me to run from the property as fast as I could. I cut behind the woodpile, lost my footing in the mud, and slid into the shed feet-first. I sat there for a minute, catching my breath. The cold rain felt good, infinite raindrops exploding off the thick canopy of trees that covered the property like a huge green parachute. I didn't mind the bad weather; in terrain I knew well, the rain would present my pursuer with an additional obstacle. I ran my fingers across my face to check for lacerations. All I felt was the dried mud still caked there from my fall.

The lights were still on up at the house. I couldn't see the man. I thought that he must have run out the front door and down the crooked dirt path to the road, not knowing that I was hiding only forty feet away.

I unzipped the bag, pulled out the small flashlight, clicked it on, and held it between my teeth. Directing the beam in front of me, I turned the spinner on the combination lock that held the wooden battery shed doors closed. I went blank. I couldn't remember the combo. Then, in a rush, it came back to me: 5-16-1. I moved the dial back and forth quickly, removed the lock, and pulled the doors open.

I focused the light on a thick red cable that ran from its connection points in between the two, large black photovoltaic batteries and then disappeared into the ground. The cable resurfaced beneath the foundation of the main building, snaking through a hole my mom had drilled through the mudroom floor. The batteries powered all the lights and appliances in the house, and once it was cut, the house would go dark immediately.

I pulled out the pocketknife from the bag and selected the largest blade. Cutting through the cable was tougher than I thought. It was reinforced with two layers: one of plastic, the other, rubber. Twice, I stopped to rest. Normally, a job like that would have taken me thirty seconds, maybe a minute; with my ribs aching, it took five minutes. With the last sawing motion of the sharp blade, the house lights flickered once and went dark. But the reality of my situation became clear to me:

I was alone in the forest. A stranger had been in the house, and he still might be. Or, he might have taken off after me. I had no way of communicating with anyone, no protection from the weather, and limited supplies. I locked up the shed and started down the south trail toward Black Creek.

Chapter V: A Dark and Desperate Run

The beam of my flashlight danced across the small streams that ran along the sides of the trail. It was muddy and slick. I half-walked, half-ran close to the ground, pushing low-hanging tree branches out of the way. Every so often, I would stop and listen for the man, but the sound of the rain made that impossible.

I'm not sure how long it took to reach Black Creek. For the first time since I had jumped through the window, the rain had stopped. A silver sliver of moon peeked out from behind a cloud, bright enough so that I could turn off my flashlight and save the batteries.

I stood and overlooked the raging torrent of water as it roared downhill. Black Creek wasn't a creek at all that winter; it was a river. Millions of gallons of water, swirling with tree branches and mud and rocks and the carcasses of dead animals, rushed past me in a deadly and powerful cascade that was as deafening as it was unstoppable. Instinctively, I stepped back. One slip meant instant death.

A rock outcropping sat ten feet from the water's edge, and I walked over to it and sat down on a smooth section that was close to horizontal but far from comfortable. The rock had another smaller flat ledge that I could use for emptying the bag. I pulled out my supplies one at a time:

One crumpled blue waterproof windbreaker;

One small first aid kit, containing four bandages, three cotton balls, a small container of iodine, a snakebite kit, and a circular mirror about one inch in diameter;

One chocolate bar, snapped in half, but with wrapper intact;

Two twelve-ounce metal bottles of drinking water;

One small wind-up AM transistor radio;

One pocket knife with three blades, bottle opener, corkscrew, Phillips and regular screwdrivers, spoon and fork;

One piece of white paper, folded into fourths.

I unfolded the paper and clicked the flashlight on:

Danny,

I hope you never have to read this. But if you are, then something has happened. I don't know what, but something. I packed this bag for you just in case. As a last resort, try to make it to the Fork. It's where Black Creek and Bull Run River come together. When you're near, you'll know it. I'm not sure if anyone's still at the Fork, at least you'll find shelter there.

In this bag won't be all the tools you'll need to face this challenge. You'll find them inside yourself. You have the strength. You know the territory. You can do it, whatever it is. I know that. I hope you know it too.

Good luck.

Mom

It was raining again. I was worried about what my mom might find when she returned to the house. And I was scared. I wiped my face with the back of my hand and took a couple of deep breaths. I had to keep going.

I gathered up the supplies and put them back in the red bag, except for the candy bar and the bottle of water. I used a stick to dig a hole and buried the bottle about six inches deep. I could always find fresh rain runoff if I needed to; getting rid of the bottle would lighten my load.

I unwrapped the candy bar like I was performing delicate surgery on a tiny patient. In the forest, food would be harder to come by than water, and I didn't want to waste even one crumb. I hadn't had anything to eat since morning, but adrenaline, and pain, had masked my hunger. As I carefully pulled half the broken candy bar from its wrapper, the smell of chocolate reminded me of how hungry I really was.

It looked so good. I imagined biting into the soft chocolate, feeling it give way, reaching the crunchy cookie in the middle of the bar. I wanted to stuff the whole piece in to my mouth but thought better of it. If the candy bar was to be the only food I would have for a while, I would have to ration.

I decided to eat one-fourth of the half I had unwrapped, then another fourth about every hour. With two halves, that would give me about eight hours to find another source of food.

The chocolate bar tasted every bit as delicious as I thought it would. Smooth. Creamy. Rich. Crunchy. I wished I had made sure before that night that the emergency bag was full of food.

A rustling in the woods startled me. The thought of food disappeared; it was back to reality. I hoped the sound was from some forest creature. I doubted that the man, with his considerable bulk, would be quick or quiet enough to sneak up on me, but it was time to move. I grabbed a pile of muddy leaves from behind the rock and spread them randomly over the entire area. In case the thief had tracking skills, I didn't want to leave any clues.

I would follow Black Creek as it wound south toward its larger and more powerful sister, Bull Run River. There were two good reasons to stay with the trail that ran parallel to the creek. The creek provided good noise cover, so I could move quickly. And, about five miles downstream, there were people who had settled at the fork of Black Creek and Bull Run River.

Chapter VI: The Story of the Forkers

When I was younger, lying in bed late at night, I used to hear the distant echo of gunshots ricocheting up the valley walls. Out in the woods, guns are not uncommon. People use them for hunting and for self-defense. Still, the sound spooked me.

"Those gunshots are coming from down near the Forkers' property," my mom would tell me. "Probably just target practice."

"The Forkers have been there a few years now," she had explained. "The community started with just one family. They moved up to escape what they felt were the negatives of the city: traffic, crime, pollution, overcrowding, poor schools.

"The couple had three children: a ten-year-old boy and twin girls seven years old. It was a tough adjustment for the kids at first - a real culture shock. They missed their friends and the conveniences of society - TV, fast food, stuff like that.

"But it didn't take long for them to grow accustomed to their new surroundings. It was exciting living out in the wild. Their dad kept them busy by having them help build the house. But it was the older boy who really flourished, learning how to hunt and fish and how to handle weapons.

"The twins became expert trackers. They learned to tell what kind of animals had been on their property, how large they were, and in what direction they were headed. Their father also taught the girls expert knife skills; they could skin and filet almost any animal their brother would bring back to the camp.

"But things were far from perfect at the Forkers' property. As the boy grew older, his dad gave him more and more responsibility. He was put in charge of the daily operations: wood-gathering for the fire, hunting, making sure the garden was producing plenty of fruits and vegetables.

"He relied on his sisters to help him with the more mundane tasks: clearing brush, fencing the perimeter of the property; jobs that were difficult and exhausting.

"In time, the twins grew tired of the endless work. They appealed to their father for help, but by this time, he had developed a debilitating disease and was too sick to help them. And as their father's health declined, their brother grew mean with his new power and was treating the girls more like slaves than sisters.

"The kids' mother died a few weeks later in a freak accident. She was swimming in a stream down-river when she stumbled on a rock, fell, and hit her head, causing bleeding in her brain.

"With their mother gone and their father bedridden and unable to speak, the brother ran the camp with an iron fist. Life for the twins was unbearable - a never-ending chain of sweaty 18-hour workdays spent dragging huge piles of brush, chopping wood, and cleaning the house. They were desperate to leave the camp but were miles away from civilization and their brother had warned them that if they tried to flee, bears would certainly track them and kill them. He also told them that if they survived the bears, he would hunt them down, bring them back, and make it even worse for them.

"The twins came up with an escape plan. In the middle of the night, they would trick their older brother by screaming that there was a bear trying to get into the house. He would grab one of the shotguns off the wall and dash outside to confront the animal. When he ran out the front door, the sisters would use a knife and a gun to force their brother to lead them out of the woods. If he refused, they would shoot him - and take their chances with the bears.

"The sisters chose a night with no moon. They both wore black. One of them hid outside the front door. From her position in the living room, the other sister suddenly screamed at the top of her lungs, 'Bear! There's a grizzly outside the door! Brother! Help! Brother!'

"A second later, a figure carrying a shotgun raced through the pitch-black living room and burst through the front door, raising the gun to his shoulder to take aim. My mom wouldn't tell me exactly what the sisters did then; it was too gory to describe.

"The girl inside the house rushed outside to join her sister. A body lay crumpled on the front porch. They rolled the body over onto its back. Something was wrong. The body was too skinny, too frail, to be their brother.

"Their father, having heard his daughter's desperate plea for help, had somehow summoned the strength to climb out of bed. He had grabbed the gun and run outside to save his daughter. As the girls' eyes adjusted to the dark, they looked down at their father's face. He was dead.

"Then, another figure appeared in the doorway, this one very much alive, a shotgun in his hands. 'Stand up,' their brother told them. 'I'm going to give you a half-hour head start. Now go.'"

"No one knows what happened to the twins or to their brother after that," my mom told me. "They were never seen again. We do know that soon after, some city cousins of the Forkers got word of the tragedy and made their way to the

19

property. Some ended up staying. We don't know how many people are at The Fork now."

I had no idea who was there or what was in store for me if I made it to the Fork. But I didn't have anywhere else to go. I made slow progress, walking in almost total darkness, stumbling over fallen branches, scraping my arms on thorny bushes. I didn't know how many hours of battery power I had left in the flashlight and I couldn't take the chance of being without light if I absolutely needed it. Even in the dark, moving in the right direction wasn't a problem. I just followed the roar of the creek.

After what must have been at least a couple of hours of hiking, I was getting tired. I stopped, opened the red bag, pulled out the windbreaker and draped it over my head and body. It wasn't raining but I was still wet, and the warmth helped a little. I sat down and took out the small pouch that contained the iodine and cotton balls and cleaned off some of the scratches on my arms.

I took another bite of chocolate. Delicious. A blade from the pocketknife made a good pick for the remaining bits of food in my teeth. It was barely anything, but I hoped it might give me at least some energy that I would need down-river.

Suddenly I was overcome by exhaustion. It was as if every muscle in my body had reached its breaking point. My head ached and my ribs throbbed from the fall. My body refused to go any further. I needed a few hours of sleep, but I knew it would be stupid to let my guard down. To be discovered asleep would be suicide. I would need the advantage of at least a few seconds warning.

I scanned the area with the flashlight, moving the shaft of light back and forth across the landscape. The beam of light seemed to magnify the roar of the creek and the buzz of the forest's nightlife that surrounded me.

The light fell across a large, tilting oak tree about 15 feet down river. Its thick branches canopied out over the water, not quite reaching the other side before they disappeared into the murky water of Black Creek. Ten feet up from its wide base, the tree split into three separate branches, each thick enough to be trees in their own right. The creek was wider and calmer here, having formed an eddy that circulated around large boulders before regaining its momentum and heading back downstream.

***

The three thick branches ascended, wrapping and twisting around each other, competing to see which could become the strongest and tallest. This sibling rivalry had created a natural bathtub-shaped pocket. It looked like a perfectly protected place to get some rest. I would be completely invisible to anyone looking up and would have the advantage of elevation. Of course, if the tree was to fall while I was in it, I would be plunged into Black Creek, drown, and be entombed in the tree. But the chance of that happening was slim and I had to take it. I scoured the ground for a few rocks, and, finding three, stood up and tossed the first one underhanded into the tree, hoping to dislodge any critters that had made the tree their home.

I threw it short and the rock bounced off the trunk, ricocheting into the creek. But my next one hit the mark, sending a pair of squirrels scampering furiously down the tree and into the woods.

I walked over to the big oak and tested the base of it with my foot. Then, digging my fingers into the spaces between the bark, I hoisted myself up. Just in time, the moon peeked through the thick, dark storm clouds. I surveyed the area and plotted an escape route in case the man found me while I slept. Then I grabbed a small fallen branch and swept the ground around the

21

tree, covering my footsteps. Finally, with sleep pulling at my eyes, I put the strap of the bag around my neck and carefully climbed up the tree.

The space I had discovered was not comfortable. The bark's jagged edges poked out at me in all directions. It was also soggy. But, lying on my back, it kind of conformed to my frame. It would have to do. Small pools of rainwater had collected in the crooked pockets of the tree. The overflow drained down into the center of the tree, which must have been hollow, because every few seconds, I heard the pop of a water droplet echo back from underneath me. It was strange, being able to hear that drop, with so many millions of gallons of water rushing by me, not a hundred feet away.

With the moon out again, I could see clearly in all directions. Just water and trees. I used the emergency bag as a pillow and covered my upper body with the windbreaker. Finally, I stuck the pocketknife into the tree next to my head. I tried to push all that had happened out of my mind. I couldn't, of course. I didn't remember falling asleep.

Chapter VII: A Sound I Knew

I woke up suddenly and for three or four seconds I didn't know where I was. Then it rushed back to me: the man, my ribs, the hunger that was twisting my stomach, my mom not knowing about any of it. And something else. Something new. A noise. A thick, scratching, scraping sound. Like wood splintering.

I didn't move. I just lay in the crook of the tree and listened. I had heard something like it before. One of my mom's metal garden tools, a claw, made that sound when I scraped bark off of pieces of wood. Whatever was making the noise must have strong claws. I had to take a look. Slowly, inch-by-inch, I moved to the edge and looked down.

Brown bear. Huge. 600 pounds at least. Tearing at the base of the tree with its powerful claws, globs of frothy slobber flying from its huge mouth. The bear knew I was there. They have an incredibly keen sense of smell. They are also excellent climbers. I don't know why the bear didn't just climb up the tree and rip me apart. Or was he sharpening his claws for his meal?

I couldn't run. I would be no match for the bear's speed and tracking skills. All I could do was wait. The bear was either going to keep ripping at the tree, leave, or climb up and attack me. It was strange, but I felt calm. I respected the bear, its beauty and power, but I didn't feel afraid. Maybe I was in shock, I don't know.

I unzipped my bag and pulled out the last pieces of chocolate. As I finished off the rest of my food supply, a breeze came up and blew the foil wrapper out of the tree, landing a few feet from the bear. The animal wandered over to it, took a sniff, turned it over once with his snout, and returned to the tree to continue his scratching. I lay back down and waited. I closed my eyes, and, somehow, went back to sleep.

I awoke with the bright morning sun burning my face. Had it all been a dream? I checked my legs to make sure the bear hadn't snacked on them while I had slept. I looked over the ledge. The animal was there, curled up, its snout buried in its belly, sound asleep.

I could throw a vine around its neck for a leash and take it for a walk. I laughed out loud at the ridiculous image. The sound was enough to wake up the bear. It raised its head and looked around, then stood, straightened its forelegs, and stretched, letting out a deep, guttural growl that sent vibrations through the tree and up through me. Then, for the first time, it looked up at me. It seemed almost tame. I wondered if the bear had been in captivity at one time. That might explain its behavior: the desire to stay close to a human, the scratching at the tree.

I knew the bear might kill me if I climbed down. But I also knew that, if I stayed in the tree, I would die of starvation or thirst. I decided to check if the bear would show aggression toward me. I moved my foot over the edge. No response. I moved my leg lower, dangling it over the edge, moving it back and forth. Nothing. I sat up and pulled my other leg over the edge. The bear sat at the base of the tree, opened its mouth wide and let out a lazy yawn. It put its head back down on the ground between its paws and looked up at me again. This animal was like an overgrown teddy bear, completely uninterested in anything I was doing. Except that it wouldn't leave.

My instincts told me that the bear wouldn't consider me prey. If I was wrong, it would be the last instinct I would ever have. I grabbed the bag and pulled the knife out of the tree bark, wrapping my hand firmly around the handle. If the bear attacked, a few well-placed thrusts at the eyes and snout might delay the inevitable for a few seconds.

I had heard stories about how some bears would play with their food for hours, dragging a carcass around the woods like a limp chew toy. If the bear was going to attack, I hoped for a quick death; maybe a razor-sharp paw swipe through my jugular vein, or a wide, bloodletting bite into my stomach.

Inch-by-inch, I lowered myself down the trunk of the tree, half-expecting to feel the hideous clamp of the bear's jaws around my leg. My back was turned to the animal. I stood at the base of the tree and turned my head to look.

The bear sat on its hind legs and regarded me with no visible emotion. I was relieved for a moment; then I remembered why I had climbed up the tree in the first place. I shivered as the cold morning sun cast its first rays across the creek. I turned away from the bear and I was on my way again - hungry, aching, but alive.

Chapter VIII: Something That Didn't Belong

The forest was a friendlier place during the day, all chirping birds and playful shadows. I found what might have been a trail, although the barely visible wisp of dirt barely qualified. I shuffled down to the edge of Black Creek and pulled a large leaf off of a plant. I folded it taco-style and scooped up cold, fresh mountain water. But by the time the leaf made it to my mouth, all that was left was a small sip. I abandoned that idea and, getting into push-up position, drank straight from the creek until my thirst was gone. Crouching at the creek's edge, I splashed water on my face, washing off some of the mud that was still caked there from my fall the previous day.

Despite my strong hunger and lack of energy, I moved pretty quickly, only stopping to rest a minute, drink, or pee. I estimated I had hiked about five hours since I had left the bear, but my fatigued brain struggled to figure out how many miles I had traveled.

As I trudged through the vegetation that grew along the bank of the creek, I thought more about the stranger. My mom said that the isolation of the forest and the lack of human contact could cause a person's mind to slip - not in a day or in a week, but over time: months, sometimes years. She had explained how living up in the mountains affected some people:

"It's like a seed that's planted without permission in your brain, Danny," she said. "It takes root and begins to grow, slowly, imperceptibly, and a person looks around at the trees and up at the sky, and listens to the sound of the forest, and, although nothing has changed, they're convinced that something is different.

"In their eyes, everything's smaller, and sharper, more...sinister. It's as if someone changed the lens on their in-

26

ternal camera, and now they're no longer sure what they're look-ing at." I wondered if what she had described had happened to the intruder. It was one more reason to stay away from him.

A huge old-growth redwood lay across my path and across Black Creek, blocking my way. It had to be 200 feet in length and thirty feet in circumference. The volume of the water was too great to make it under the tree and had backed up and formed a swirling cauldron, churning violently with broken branches and other trapped debris.

I was about to open up the bag again when something on the other side of the creek caught my eye. Maybe a hundred feet away, it instantly registered as a color that didn't belong: neon orange. Just a small blur of it, obscured by thick vegetation, in-visible if I didn't focus on it and move my head a few inches left or right. I was confident that the color was from something that wasn't alive. Or natural. I wanted to take a closer look, so with some effort, I crawled out of the root pit and pulled myself up onto the big tree. Extending my arms for balance, I began a care-ful tightrope walk across its slippery surface, the massive tree vibrating and shifting under me. Black Creek was straining to push its massive, unwanted visitor out of the way, and I was a passenger along for the ride. My foot slipped on a mossy patch, but I caught myself and regained my balance.

Once on the other side of the creek I made the long leap down off the tree and began searching for the color. Pulling the sleeves of my windbreaker down over my hands for protection, I swept my arms back and forth across large plant fronds, moving them out of the way.

Then, there it was, out of the undergrowth: a rusty, rectangu-lar piece of sheet metal, maybe two by three feet, attached to a three-foot length of pipe that was buried in the ground. Vines crept around and over it. I ripped some of them away.

It was a sign, the border neatly painted neon orange. The block letters looked like they had been traced by stencil. How disconcerting it was, in a forest of crazy angles and chaotic unpredictability, to see words so perfectly straight and black against the rusty metal:

TRESPASSERS: YOU ARE ENTERING
PRIVATE PROPERTY.
TURN BACK NOW.
FRANK.

I stepped back and looked at the ground around the sign. Except for the leaves that my own footsteps had trampled, it didn't look like anyone had been there.

Frank. Maybe he lived at the Fork, at the community that my mom had mentioned in her letter. I hoped so; I needed help. I couldn't travel much longer on my own. And then I smelled the odor of burning wood, of a fireplace, and I thought I might be close to getting help and felt a burst of energy.

Sometimes I look back and wonder what would have happened if I had just turned around and gone back the other way, like the sign had suggested. How might my life have been different? How might have yours, Justin? But I ignored the sign's warning and took off down what was a clearly defined trail that grew wider the farther and faster I walked. And then I heard it. Or actually, felt it.

The ground was shaking. It was as if I was standing on the top of a giant stereo speaker except that there was no volume, only a constant, deep vibration that began at my feet and ran through my legs and up into my ribcage. Of course. The Fork! The place where Black Creek and its big sister, Bull Run River, met in a violent collision that literally shook the ground around it.

28

"Don't move or I'll shoot."

The voice came from behind me. I froze, silently cursing myself for allowing someone to sneak up on me when I had made it this far.

"Get down on your knees." I did.

Maybe it was from lack of sleep or from hunger or adrenaline, but I felt calm, considering that someone I couldn't see was apparently pointing a gun at me.

"Throw the bag behind you."

I unwrapped the strap from my wrist and tossed the bag back over my head.

"Clench your fingers together and put your hands behind your head," the voice said. "Don't turn around or I will discharge the weapon."

I did what he told me and felt the scratchy burn of thick rope on my wrists as my hands were tied together.

"I guess you can't read, kal-san-gip."

"What do you mean?"

I knew he was talking about the sign. But I figured the more we spoke, the better the chances I would have of surviving the encounter. I wondered what that word meant that he had called me: "kal-san-gip."

"I saw you read the sign." There was no emotion in his voice. It was like the monotone voice from a robot in an old science fiction movie.

"What sign? I don't know what you're talking about," I lied.

"Yes you do. Stand up."

I struggled to my feet, almost losing my balance, but managing to keep my hands behind my head.

"Start walking, zah-tah-juh."

I felt a sharp poke in the back. I had never felt the business end of a gun, but I figured that's what it felt like. I started walking. The trail was almost as wide as a narrow one-lane dirt road now. Frequent jabs in the back, more annoying than painful, reminded me to keep my pace up. *Kal-san-gip. Zah-tah-juh.* I don't know why, but it felt important to remember the strange words he was using.

"Where are we going?" I asked.

"Shut up," came the answer.

The burning wood smell was stronger now. The sound of the rushing water grew louder. Fifty yards down the path, I saw it.

The Fork. It was like a volcano, except instead of molten lava, it was white water that was erupting, spewing thirty feet into the air. A gray fog of heavy mist was beginning to soak my clothes. Black Creek ran angry after a storm, but Bull Run River's temper made her little sister seem like a timid child.

Maybe in some alternate universe I would have tried to pull the rope off my hands and dive into the water, cover my head with my arms, dodge the hundreds of tons of deadly debris rushing past until the current pulled me safely down river. But that was just a fantasy. The gun pressed against my back was reality. We kept walking, didn't speak.

The trees and vegetation became less dense. We came to the top of a hill. A pile of bricks, maybe a pallet's worth, was neatly stacked, the sides so smoothly aligned that at first it looked like a solid slab of concrete. We headed downhill. Firewood. Chopped fir, birch, and ash lined the next section of the path. The piles were stacked so that the edges of the pieces were lined up close to perfect. Weird. Other piles were tarped and protected from the elements; the edges of the green plastic sheets formed 90-degree angles. There had to be at least a couple of years supply of firewood.

The path became a dirt road. It veered left and then sloped uphill again. The elevation peaked and we started heading downhill. To the right, on a plateau that seemed too flat to be naturally formed, sat a large, well-tended garden: carrots, peppers, beans, tomatoes, many other vegetables, and a large section for flowers. To the left of the garden, there was a small tool shed. Past the shed, at the top of the grade, sat a house.

I wasn't sure if I was looking at the front or back of it. Stairs had been cut directly into the dirt that led up to a wide deck that was protected by a redwood fence framed with brass banisters. Large, ornately stained windows guarded both sides of a glass door that was framed with wood. The roof was sloped unusually steep and held eight or ten solar panels.

A large black dog, maybe pit bull labrador mix, bounded down the stairs, directly toward me. Instinctively I turned away, not knowing if he was going to attack. He jumped up on me a couple times and spun hyper-excited circles in the dirt in front of me.

"Down, dog, dammit!" yelled my captor. "Ignore him." After my stressful and exhausting time in the woods, the dog's antics were welcome relief. A woman's voice called down from the direction of the house. I couldn't see her through the trees next to the stairs, but she had a friendly tone.

"Now, Frank, you know Acer can't help it! He loves people. Who have you got there?"

"I found him snooping in the forest up by the sign," the young man said, his deep voice full of suspicion. "I brought him in for questioning, see if he knows anything."

"Frank Summers!" the lady yelled in a shrill voice, "you let that boy's hands free this instant and bring him inside! And put that gun back in the shed!"

"Aww, Mama!" he bellowed, his voice full of whiny disappointment. "He was *trespassing*!" The rope loosened. I was able to drop my arms in front of me. I shook out my hands, trying to get some circulation back.

Then I turned around to look at the person who had held me at gunpoint. He was walking away, his back turned to me. My red bag was in one hand and, in the other, a pistol. He entered the shed and reappeared a second later, still carrying my bag but without the gun.

He was a few inches taller than me, and wider, too. He had on jeans and muddy hiking boots, and a tight, military-style camouflage t-shirt that showed the muscles in his arms and chest. His face was wide, with a square jaw. Intense, distrustful brown eyes peered out from under a dirty green baseball cap pulled low over his brow. I guessed he was about fifteen. He walked up to me and held out my bag.

"I guess this is yours," he said, under his breath. I reached out to take it from him but he pulled it away suddenly and then thrust it into my chest with a push, knocking me backward.

"Don't get too comfortable here," he told me, with a quiet anger that seemed to bubble from inside of him like molten lava. He looked up at the house and then looked back at me. "Go on up."

I began walking up the stairs. My legs felt like cement. The high-strung dog alternated frenetically between leading the way and returning to lick my hands. With effort, I made it up to the deck, but by then my head felt thick and my thoughts were clouded. The door was open. I stepped inside. The woman was there.

"You don't look good," she said. "Come sit down."

I walked over to the couch and sat. After the night in the tree and the forced hike, it felt good. No, it felt great. The woman sat down in a brown rocking chair across from me. She handed me a glass of water and I took a sip.

I looked at her. It was hard to tell her age, but I thought maybe forty. She had on corduroy pants and a brown t-shirt and no shoes. Her hair was equal parts gray and black, tied behind her head in a messy ponytail.

"First off," she said, "I want to apologize about Frank. He means well but he's become a little overprotective in the time he's been up here. It can happen."

"That's OK," I answered.

"Now," she continued, "who are you, and what are you doing on our property?"

I sat back. What did she ask me? Who, and...what? I couldn't organize my thoughts. I started talking anyway.

"My name is Danny Tyme. I'm your neighbor from about, I don't know, five or ten miles back up, uh, where? Oh, up toward Black Creek. My mom left. I had an accident. Two days ago...no, I mean, yesterday - wait, when?"

My vision was blurring, getting fuzzy on the sides. The time I had spent in the forest, being hungry and hurt and exhausted, had caught up to me. My mouth was dry and sticky. Black spots crept into my vision. I heard a voice that sounded as if it was echoing from deep inside a tunnel:

"Are-are-you-you-you-OK-OK-OK-OK?"

Chapter IX: Mama's Place

I could sense the morning before my eyes opened. For a second, I was at peace. Then the reality of everything that had happened during the last two days came flooding back and filled me with dread.

I sat up. I was on the couch and covered with a rough wool blanket. Sunlight streamed through one of the stained-glass windows, blurring a patch of hardwood floor with fuzzy reds and blues and greens.

I felt better; my ribs weren't as sore. I touched my face; it was clean. The woman must have washed it while I slept. I stood up and folded the blanket. I didn't look at the inside of the house. Instead, I went outside, quietly sliding closed the glass door behind me.

It was warm. The sky was clear. I took a deep breath and closed my eyes, trying to wake up in my own bed and realize all of it had been a nightmare. That didn't happen. I looked out past the garden and beyond the bluff. The view was amazing. The property dropped off suddenly, revealing unending miles of lush green forest. Bull Run River, so violent and powerful the night before, now snaked silently through the forest, disappearing into the haze at the edge of the horizon. Massive gray pillows of fog filled in the spaces between the mountains.

I stood on the deck, waiting for some ingenious plan to materialize in my brain. None did. I didn't know what to do. I went back inside and sat down. I felt alone. The dog was at my feet. Acer. He was calmer than yesterday. He licked my hand and looked up at me, panting. He seemed to know something was wrong. Dogs sense that stuff, I think. I scratched his head. He stood up and walked to the door, pawing it a few times. Then he returned and nudged my hand.

I got up and opened the door a few inches. He squeezed outside and raced down the stairs. At the bottom, he looked back up, as if to make sure I was following him. Seeing I wasn't, he bounded back up. This time, he walked down only a couple of stairs before turning around.

"What is it, Acer?" I asked him. "What do you want?"

Spurred on by the question, the dog burst down the stairs and toward the shed, the little building where Frank had stored his gun after releasing me as a hostage. Acer scratched at the shed door twice and then spun around to see if I was coming.

I walked over to the shed. Acer was standing at attention, body stiff but tail wagging expectantly, his snout an inch from the door. The door wasn't closed completely. I pushed on it and it squeaked open.

On a chipped wooden countertop sat a bag of dog treats. I reached into the shed just far enough to open the bag and pull out a treat.

I told Acer to sit. He didn't. He just stood there, eyes focused on the treat, apparently trying to impress me with his extraordinary canine patience. I gave in. He snapped the treat from my hand and bolted from the shed, sprinted past the garden, and bounded back up the steps.

I pushed the shed door all the way open. On the wall to my left hung what looked like gold miners' gear: pans, picks, rock hammers, buckets, kerosene lamps, headgear, kneepads, flashlights. The gun was hanging by its strap from a nail.

Built into the wall on the right above the countertop was a large square-shaped opening, framed with 2x4s, through which the entire valley was visible. It seemed to me that whomever had built the shed had intended to put glass in it; maybe they realized they didn't need it.

"He'll come back for another. He always does." The voice came from beneath the big cutout.

I leaned over the counter and stuck my head out of the wooden square. There was a girl there, standing in trampled brush near a table full of seedling trays that were under a glass enclosure held up by a branch. She was ripping pieces of tape off a roll, sticking them on to black plastic trays and labeling them with a pen. Lettuce, sprouts, alfalfa, broccoli. She didn't look up.

"Who will come back?" I asked her.

"Acer," she said. "Once you give him a treat, he runs up the stairs, eats it, and comes back down for another."

"He's not back yet," I replied.

"He will be," she said. And then there he was, standing next to me.

"This is one of my favorite places," the girl said, looking up at me.

She had short dark hair and almond-shaped brown eyes and dimples, but it was her black lipstick that I noticed most. I had never seen that before. I thought she might have been about 14 years old. Behind her, the sun's late-morning rays cast horizontal shadows on the trees, illuminating buzzing clouds of insects.

"It's peaceful here," she continued, returning to her labeling. "Just me and the plants." I didn't know if she was trying to tell

me that she wanted to be alone. But she had started the conversation.

"So, where am I?" I asked her.

"Mama's place," she said. "I figured you knew, since...well,
since you're *here*. It's been a while since we've had a new kid."

"Oh, I'm not staying," I told her. "Something happened up
at my place. I fell and got hurt. My mom was gone, and she
didn't know. I'm just looking for help."

"Yeah, we all have our stories," she said. "Mine, it's pretty
simple: my parents just couldn't handle me. So, they brought
me here, to Mama."

"So this is a group home?" I asked her. "And Mama is in
charge?"

"Kinda," she said, blowing a lock of hair away from her
face. "Except that there are no fences or gates here, nothing to
keep you from leaving. Mama takes kids in and gives 'em food
and shelter in exchange for work around the property. That's
pretty much it. Oh, and sometimes meetings about chores."

"What do you mean, your parents couldn't handle you?" I
blurted. I already regretted asking her.

"You don't even know my name," the girl said, softly.

"You're right," I said. "Sorry. I'm Danny. Danny
Tyme. What's yours?"

The girl looked beyond the shed, up toward the house. Her
voice turned to a whisper.

"My name's Desiree. We can talk later." She picked up a tray and carried it to the garden. I turned to leave. Frank was standing in the doorway. I don't know how long he had been there, or what he had heard.

"What are you doing in here, kap-seese?" That word again.

"I was just - getting Acer a treat."

"That's *my* dog," he said. "And *my* shed. And *my* girl-friend." Frank's angry words echoed down toward the garden. I couldn't see Desiree but she must have been listening. "There's a lot you better learn around here in a hurry, boy."

"Listen," I said, trying for a fresh start, "I'm not going to be around here long, OK? I just need to get back up to my place and I'll be out of your hair."

"Yeah, I heard that story you told Mama," he said. "What a crock. Why don't you just admit it? Nobody wants you. You're lucky Mama took you in." A bell sounded up at the house.

Frank slammed the shed door on me. I waited for a second, took a breath, and pushed it open. He was almost up the stairs, heading into the house. Desiree appeared again. "The bell means chow time," she said.

"Why is he so - "

She raised her finger to her lips to cut me off, shaking her head.

"Not now," she whispered. "I'll walk up alone," she said. "You come up a few minutes later."

When I got inside, Frank and Desiree were already at the table. Mama was in the kitchen, putting chicken, mashed potatoes
and veggies onto plates.

"Wash up before you eat, Danny," Mama told me. "Head
down the hall and you'll see the bathroom." Frank tracked me
with his eyes as I walked past him. Desiree didn't look up.

Halfway down the hall, a door on the left was open. I
peeked in. It was a disaster. The bed covers were on the
floor. Papers were scattered on top of them. A plant was tipped
over on the desk. There was writing on the wall. No time to
read it.

The next room down was the opposite. The bed was made
with military precision. Tight corners, the blanket so smooth
that it looked like plastic. There was a desk with nothing on it, a
chair tucked underneath. The closet was open. Shoeboxes were
stacked inside, their edges squared off to form a cube. It reminded me of the woodpiles I had seen on the way to the
house. I found the bathroom, washed my hands, and returned
to the table.

I was starving. I took a few big bites and looked up. Desiree
was poking at her mashed potatoes with a fork. She hadn't eat-
en a thing. Next to her plate was a little paper cup. I didn't look
at Frank, but I couldn't help notice what was going on with his
plate. He had squared off his mashed potatoes. The pile was
perfect - about a half-inch tall and three by three inches
square. Tight corners. The green beans were pushed together
and lined up parallel to each other, like a little green raft. Two
beans had been discarded off of the plate, apparently rejected
because they were bent.

Frank couldn't seem to figure out what to do with his piece
of chicken. First, he had it isolated on the plate, away from the

40

other food. Then, he stabbed it with his knife and laid it on top of the bed of green beans, but that caused some of the beans to move. He removed the chicken and placed it on a napkin next to his plate, then repaired the raft of green beans. I pretended not to notice any of this.

"So, Danny, welcome," Mama said, looking at Frank and Desiree to see if they might take the cue and say something similar. Neither did.

"From what you described yesterday, it sounds like you've been through quite an ordeal. We're glad you're safe and once you get your strength back, I'm sure Frank will be happy to help you get back to your property safely and wait with you until your mom returns."

"I never said I would help him!" Frank shot back at Mama, dropping his silverware onto his plate with a crash. "I just said I'd point him in the right direction!" He looked at me with a disgusted scowl.

"Frank Summers!" Mama shouted. "While Danny is here, he is a member of our family and is to be treated with kindness and respect! You follow me into the kitchen right now." Frank looked defeated. He stood up and started off to the kitchen, shoulders slumped. After a few steps, he turned and glared at me, as if to say, "I'll get you for this!"

Mama and Frank walked through the kitchen and into what was a small laundry room or pantry. I couldn't hear any of the words, but she was doing the talking. Mama's head was tilted to the side and she was pointing at Frank. He stood, looking down, hands in his pockets.

"Danny." Desiree was whispering at me.

"Yeah?"

"Meet me at the shed tonight, about an hour after lights out. I want to tell you something."

"What is it?" I asked her.

"Can you keep a secret?" she asked.

"Yeah, sure." I said it without thinking; the reality was that no one had ever asked me to keep a secret.

"Then just meet me there."

"What about Frank?" I asked. "He told me not to go into the shed anymore. He said it was his."

"Frank likes to think he runs this place," she answered. "But he doesn't. It's a community. We all have rights." She said it with quiet confidence, like she had gotten into hassles with Frank before and hadn't backed down.

"What if he comes down there?" I asked.

"One thing about Frank," she said, "is that he's a real deep sleeper. Once he's in his room, you can pretty much forget it. He'll be out for the night."

Frank and Mama returned to the table, Frank eyeballing me as he slowly pulled his chair out and sat down.

"So, Danny," Mama started again, "I know you probably won't be around here very long. Still, you should know a few things about how the house works. First thing is, everybody contributes. Each resident has a job. Without everyone's help, the house and the property can't run smoothly. My job is to cook, clean the kitchen, and keep the bathrooms neat. Desiree, why don't you share with Danny what your job is?"

"I take care of the garden," Desiree said, her face lighting up. "I run the composting operation, prepare the soil, plant, and harvest." She seemed to take pride in her work.

"And Frank?" Mama asked, turning to him. 'What are *your* responsibilities?"

An awkward pause. Then Frank grimaced, closed his eyes, and exhaled slowly, like Mama was inflicting great pain by forcing him to join the conversation.

"I make sure there's enough wood to keep the fire going," he said in his too-deep voice, annoyed. "I also *fix* anything that breaks around here. And most importantly, I'm in charge of security. Every day I patrol the property and make sure the perimeter is secure. You never know what you might find *slithering* nearby." He looked at me. Mama ignored the comment.

"So, Danny," she said, "there's still some vegetables to be harvested, but our biggest need right now is garden prep. While you're here, why don't you help Desiree with that? You can take over compost duty while she focuses on harvest."

"Ok."

I wasn't sure what my job would actually be, but I hoped it wouldn't be anywhere near Frank. His negative energy and anger was something I could only handle in short spurts. On the other hand, it would be nice if I were working close to Desiree. It sounded like from Mama's description that we'd both be around the garden.

I looked over at Desiree but couldn't see her eyes. She was busy braiding three thick strands of hair in front of her face, overlapping them, and then letting them spin loose and starting over.

"I'd also like you to tag along with Frank on his patrol around the property," Mama said to me. "It's never a bad thing to have two sets of eyes out there."

The idea of bringing me along on the security hike was apparently just too much for Frank to deal with. He stood up, used two hands to push in his chair, and stared at me. I was sure he was going to say something, but he didn't.

He left, walking through the kitchen and into the mudroom, the side entry into the house used for shedding wet clothes and muddy shoes. There was a doggy door for Acer as well. Frank stood in the mudroom for a second, then opened the door, walked out, and slammed it closed.

Desiree and I cleared the table, scraping the uneaten vegetables into a bin and handing the plates to Mama to wash. Desiree walked down the hall to the messy room and paused in front of the door, looking back at me with her eyebrows raised. It was a reminder.

"Danny," Mama said, "you never told me what exactly happened up at your place." Her back was to me while she spoke. She was washing the plates by hand in a soapy pot of water, rinsing them, and then lining them up to dry in a wooden dish drainer.

"My mom had just left our property to go into town for supplies," I told her. "It was going to take her two days, there and back. It was the first time she had left me alone at the house."

"That's a lot of responsibility for a kid your age," Mama responded. "How did you feel about it?"

"I was fine with it," I said. "I had a plan for what to eat, what to do. I wasn't nervous."

"But something went wrong. What was it?" Mama finished up the dishes. She dried her hands on a dishtowel and tossed it onto the counter.

"I was at the woodpile," I said. "My mom had just left. I grabbed one too many pieces and lost my balance. I fell, and the wood fell on top of me. I must have lost consciousness."

"And then?"

"I was out for a while, because when I came to, it was dark. I was back in the house and in a lot of pain. There was a man there."

"A man?" Mama asked. "Did you know him?"

"Nope, never saw him before," I continued. "It didn't make any sense, this guy being there. He made food in the kitchen and ate. I pretended to be unconscious. Then I crawled into my mom's room and smashed a window and got out of there."

"Did he chase you?" she asked.

"I don't know," I said. It was the first time I had considered the possibility that he hadn't. "I thought he had, but I'm not sure. Anyway, I cut the power to the house and took off."

Frank re-entered through the mudroom, took off his boots and jacket, and walked to the sink to wash his hands. Mama returned to the dining room and was wiping down the table, leaving me and Frank alone.

"Still telling stories, kap-seese?" he asked me, quietly.

"Why would I lie?" I asked him. "You think I *want* to be here?" It was loud enough that Mama had to have heard. Dumb. She had been so kind to me. The last thing I wanted to do was to hurt her feelings or seem unappreciative.

"You better watch your mouth," Frank said back. "I found you in the woods, and I can put you back there."

"Why do you hate me so much?" I blurted. "You don't know me." For a split second he looked surprised. Then came a cold, blank stare, one I had seen from him before. I felt a little safer knowing Mama was there. Then I looked toward the dining room and realized she was gone.

"Yes, I do," Frank said, almost spitting the words. "I do know you. Warrant Officer told me all about your kind."

"Who is Warrant Officer?"

"Warrant Officer was a great man," he said. "You're not even worthy of speaking his name."

The words were different than any I had heard from him. No anger. It was something closer to sadness. Or emptiness.

Acer bounded in from the mudroom, his tail wagging, breathing hard. He had that manic energy dogs have after they've chased something but failed to catch it, like he was saying, "You wouldn't believe what I almost caught!" He ambled past Frank and over to me. I reached down to scratch his head.

"Acer, no!" Frank yelled. "Get over here!"

Instantly, Acer's head and body dropped down, almost to the floor. His tail stopped wagging and fell limp between his legs. He cowered over to Frank, almost sliding along the floor.

"Acer, sit!" he commanded. The dog looked over at me as if he was asking, "What did I do to deserve this?" He sat.

"Acer, lie down!" Why did Frank have to yell if the dog was already following commands? Acer lay down on his stomach, putting his head on his front paws. I felt sorry for him.

"What did I tell you about the dog?" Frank asked me.

"You said he was yours."

"That's right, zah-tah-juh. He *is* mine," he said, pointing at Acer. "A dog can only have one master."

"I don't want to be his master," I said. "I just wanted to pet him."

"Dogs don't need affection," Frank said, walking over to the sink. Acer saw his opportunity; he sprinted into the mudroom and out the doggy door. Frank didn't notice or didn't care.

"Dogs are beasts. Beasts designed to serve human beings," he continued. "We give them food, water and shelter. That's it."

Frank picked up the kitchen towel that Mama had left wadded up on the counter. He straightened it out over the sink, twice making slight adjustments to it before he was convinced that it was even with the edge.

"I'm going to bed," he said. "Tomorrow you'll come with me on my perimeter hike. I'm only taking you because Mama asked me to." He walked down the hall and disappeared into the darkness, his last words a warning: "Remember what I told you earlier."

I heard a door close. I remembered what he had told me. About the shed. And about Desiree. And the dog. And in an hour, I was going to be talking to Desiree in the shed. And Acer would probably be there too, looking for a treat.

I really hoped Frank was a deep sleeper.

Chapter X: The Tree Clock

I got to the shed before Desiree. I wasn't about to get caught inside of it, in case Frank was lurking. Instead, I walked around to the other side, where she had placed flats of germinating seeds on the worktables. From there, the ground sloped away and the trail continued down toward the valley. I took the trail. The smell of good rich soil told me that the compost pile was close. I walked for a bit. When I looked back up all I could see was the outline of the roof of the house. The crickets' chirping got louder.

Through some thick branches overhead, a small, very faint star caught my eye. I had to blink a few times just to make sure it was there. I didn't know why I would even notice it.

"Danny?"

I scrambled back up the trail and approached the shed. There was a light on inside, a single bulb that swayed, pendulum-like, and seemed to get brighter the closer I got. Desiree was leaning out the big cutout window, a shadowy silhouette.

"We're going for a walk," she said, her voice equal parts bossy and friendly. "Come around and help me."

I walked up and around. The door was open. Desiree had on a pair of jeans tucked into rubber boots, a black turtleneck sweater, and a trench coat. Her hair was pinned back and out of her face. She handed me a shovel and a scuffed up yellow helmet with a light attached to the front.

"Put the headgear on, but don't turn on the light yet," she told me. "Where we're going, it'll be dark."

49

"Darker than it already is?" I asked.

Desiree ignored me and grabbed a treat for Acer. The dog snapped it from her and bolted up the stairs. She put her helmet on, reached up and pulled the chain to turn off the shed light, and we were outside again.

She started off in front of me on the same trail that Frank had forced me to march, except in the opposite direction. My legs seemed to have rebounded since the run from my house back up the valley. Good thing, because Desiree walked fast. We passed the woodpiles and soon afterward, the road became a trail again.

"Where are we going?" I asked her.

Strands of Desiree's hair had gotten loose from her ponytail and were falling down over her face. She turned around to look at me but didn't say anything. Then she smiled and I felt something new inside of me, happy and nervous mixed together.

"You ask a lot of questions, don't you?"

"I'm just curious," I replied.

"It's not far," she said. "Maybe fifteen minutes. Into thicker forest now. Turn on your light."

I reached up and felt for the button on the battery pack. I pressed it, and a solid, bright cone of light shined against the trees. It wasn't at all like a flashlight; the beam was stronger and more focused and didn't seem to dissipate much with distance.

"Why don't we just use flashlights?" I asked.

"We'll need our hands free."

She clicked on her light. Our beams chased each other in and out of the branches. When someone has a light strapped to their head, you know what they're looking at, but not necessarily where they're going. I learned quickly that the best way to keep a consistent light on the path was to keep my head still and not look left or right too often.

A dark figure sprinted past me. Acer had finished his treat, caught up with us, and seemed excited at the idea of a nighttime walk. The forest became denser. Our pace slowed. Then Desiree stopped.

"Ok, we're here."

We were inside of a circle of trees, ten of them. Each tree was about 25 feet away from the one directly across from it, like a massive, unmoving clock, planted too precisely to be some coincidence of nature. A circular-ish patch of scrub brush sat in the center of the circle. Judging by the thickness of the trunks, I guessed the trees were planted 150 years ago. Parallel shadows cast by the trees felt alien and out of place.

Desiree grabbed the shovel from me, walked to the center, and with a solid shove of her foot, slid the business end of the shovel into the ground at the edge of the scrub patch. Then she took off her trench coat and wadded it up, placing it about ten feet away.

"Let me see your helmet," she said.

I took it off and handed it to her. She positioned the helmet on top of the trench coat so that the beam of light lit up the patch of shrub. Then she pulled the shovel out of the dirt and began to dig. Actually, "dig" isn't the right word for what she was doing. She was chopping, slicing, around the edges of the shrubby center island of the circle. I knew she already thought I asked too many questions. I asked anyway.

"What are you doing?"

"Digging, Einstein."

There was a pause. I couldn't see her face, but I think she was looking at me. And she laughed. It felt like some sort of magic elixir. It made me forget that I had been knocked unconscious and that there had been a strange man in my house, and that my mom wouldn't know where I was.

The shaft of light from my helmet caught Desiree's boot and shovel in occasional pulses as she continued to stab her way around the circumference of the clump, loosening dirt along the outside and then stepping to the left and pushing the shovel back in. The cone of light rolled onto the base of a tree; my helmet had shifted and fallen off its perch. I replaced the helmet and redirected the light back onto Desiree's shovel. Except she wasn't holding it anymore - it was stuck in the ground.

"Come here."

I walked to the center. Desiree reached under one side of the patch and pulled out a thick rope handle that had been hidden underneath. I reached under the other side and grabbed a second handle.

"Get a good grip."

"Ok, I have one."

"Now lift," she instructed. "Slowly."

The entire patch of scrub, dirt and all, lifted from its resting place. It was one big puzzle piece made out of dirt and weeds, and it was really heavy. Clumps of dirt that clung to the root system swung back and forth underneath the patch. The way Desiree handled the patch made me think we were not supposed to let any of the clumps fall. We set it down between two trees and walked back to the center.

We sat in the middle of the circle, our legs hanging down into the now empty disc-shaped space the shrub clump used to occupy. It was like a fire pit, maybe two feet deep, except that there was no fire. Desiree's light was focused on the bottom of the hole, on a scratched up, rectangular container that was covered with a layer of light brown, loose dirt. She reached down and pulled it free, tilted it on its side, brushed the dirt off and blew some of the dust off.

It was metal. The words "Electric Train Set" were printed across the top, above a punctured image of a black locomotive. On one side, a rusty rip in the metal had sliced a blue boxcar in half. The smaller text on the other side had been obliterated by moisture and time, except for the phrase, "Hours of Fun for the Whole Family!"

Desiree popped the top off and put it down next to her. She reached in and pulled out a thin silver chain. Attached to it were two small rectangular plates. Each was about the size of my thumb.

"They're called dog tags," she said.

She handed them to me. There were actually two chains. One was large and ran through a small hole in one of the tags. The smaller chain was attached to the first chain, with its own tag.

"What are they for?" I asked.

"They're identification," she said. "Every U.S. soldier wears them. The big chain goes around your neck. If you're wounded or killed, they pull the smaller chain off of the larger one, along with the tag. Take a look."

She lit up the tags with her light and handed them to me. I turned one of them over. Pressed into the metal:

SUMMERS,

FRANKLIN A.

5160152868

B POS

NO RELIGIOUS PREF

"Whose are these?"

"The tags belonged to Army Warrant Officer Franklin Summers," she said. "He wore them in Vietnam. But they're Frank's now."

Warrant Officer. You're not worthy of speaking his name.

"Warrant Officer is Frank's dad?"

"Yep."

"Why isn't his dad still wearing them?"

"Because he's dead."

Chapter XI: Warrant Officer's Letters

Desiree took the dog tags from me and put them back in the box. She pulled out a thin stack of clipped-together envelopes, then she clicked off her light. Her words materialized from the dark.

"The letters are from Warrant Officer Franklin Summers, written to his son, Frank, from Vietnam," she said. "The first one is dated 1971. That was his first year in-country."

"In-country?" I asked.

"Inside Vietnam, during the war," she explained. "Warrant Officer Summers was a helicopter pilot attached to a medevac, or medical evacuation unit. His unit delivered troops into the war zone, and then waited while wounded soldiers were loaded into the chopper for evacuation. After two months in-country, he wrote the first letter."

"Does Frank know these are here?" I asked.

"Of course," she said. "He buried them here."

"How do you know?"

"I followed him. And watched." She said it matter-of-factly.

"Why?"

It might have been a second of silence. Maybe a minute. Maybe five minutes. For the first time, I realized just how dark it was. The darkness got louder the longer she didn't answer.

Click.

Her face was lit up from beneath her chin, mouth agape, eyes wide, like in a horror movie. Supposed to be scary but funny instead. I forgot where I was.

"You want me to read a letter to you?"

"Sure."

Letter #1

10/4/71
Camp Radcliffe
An Khe Vietnam

We are huge buzzing metal horses rising against a dirty orange sky, a thousand warm mornings of dust billowing beneath our wings. We are blades and guns, ripping air and sky. We are iron and death.

You are young.

I am the lead horse, an animal fast and brave who takes the others into places that no living creature should ever go and then tries to get out without dying, or worse, getting caught.

I am far from you.

Around me, horses falter and fall, swallowed silently by the infinite forest's ancient green. Someday, the forest below us will not even hold a faint memory of our ridiculous machines.

I miss you.

Letter #2

10/25/71
Camp Radcliffe
An Khe Vietnam

We are the Original People of North America. We are The People Who Walked Out of the Woods. The Others tried to give us a name because of how we looked, but we did not accept that name. The Others pushed their culture and traditions on us. We did not accept them. Some people who looked at us saw teepees and feathers, face paint and fire dances. Some of that was real; elders still share stories of what our ancestors' lives were like many years ago, before the Others came.

We are the Original People of North America. We are the trees and mountains and water. We are the raindrops in the clouds, the wind in the trees, the land beneath your feet.

When I return from this place, I will teach you all that I learned from my father and that he learned from his. For generations it has been this way, and soon it will be time for you and me to add our link to an unbroken chain.

Important above all else is a challenge you must undertake. Its successful completion will usher you from childhood to adulthood. I will describe it in an upcoming letter. It is called Yitcarese.

Letter #3

11/14/71
Camp Radcliffe
An Khe Vietnam

Growing up, our lives had two halves. There was town, small and safe. Everyone was there: family, friends, and neighbors. Everything we needed. There wasn't a reason to leave. Town was good, and light, and safe.

The other half of our lives, the dark half, was the mountains. They were forbidden, a dangerous place where if you got lost, you might not make it home. As my friends and I got older, the mountains beckoned, called to us. We would challenge the mountains, tease them, venturing into the foothills to play. Sometimes we'd go all the way to the river. But no matter how daring and brave we got, we always made sure we could see the Witch's Nose, a spindly, bent rock outcropping that stuck out of the top of a tall ridge. If we could see the Witch's Nose, we knew we could make it home. The angle from which we saw it allowed us to determine which way to walk. The Witch's Nose was our lifeline to safety.

When I turned 14 years old, my mother and father decided that I should leave the tiny, one-room schoolhouse where I had been informally educated and go off to public school in Bend, Oregon.

The transition was a shock. I didn't know anyone. The school was huge. Classes were large. Teachers were strict. I struggled to stay organized, to keep up with all the work. I was put in a class for kids who needed extra support. I guess it was a consequence of the less-than-rigorous academic environment at the schoolhouse. I resented the help at first; I didn't want to be different than the other kids. But eventually

I realized I needed it, and I embraced it. Despite being behind when I arrived, I quickly got up to speed and excelled academically.

There were a few kids at school who identified themselves as members of our tribe, so it felt natural to hang out with them. We spent time together, studying and relaxing, and we grew close. But among the other students, we felt like outcasts. When we walked by them in the halls, they became silent. As we passed them, we could hear them whispering. None of them talked to me in class.

At that time, I was still blissfully unaware that people sometimes judged others by the color of their skin, or where they were from, or what they believed. Maybe some of it was our fault, for not reaching out and trying to relate and make new friends.

Student groups had formed on campus in support of or against the Vietnam War. I hadn't been very aware of world events, especially a war that was taking place on the other side of the world, in Southeast Asia. It didn't seem to affect me. Many seniors were registering with the Selective Service. I had heard that some kids were taking off to Canada to avoid serving.

A year later, just after graduation, I enlisted in the U.S. Army. My friends thought I was crazy: why would I risk my life fighting in a conflict on the other side of the world? I still ask myself that question. Maybe I wanted a challenge. Or maybe it was my way of trying to belong, trying to be accepted by the people who turned their backs to me in the hallways.

Letter #4

12/17/71
Camp Radcliffe
An Khe Vietnam

I went to basic training in Fort Benning, Georgia. It was summer in the south. I struggled to acclimate to the heat and humidity. The drill sergeants screamed at us. They didn't let us sleep much. We learned to fight hand-to-hand, learned how to clean, assemble, and break down weapons. We ran obstacle courses, did thousands of push-ups, and drilled constantly, marching for miles over challenging terrain. I pushed my body to its physical limits and beyond.

Once a day our drill sergeant would inspect our dormitory. It was the living area in which we slept and kept our personal belongings. Storage lockers had to be organized a certain way: shirts hung straight, contents folded precisely inside drawers, shoes lined up and tucked underneath. Even the soap, shampoo and toothpaste had an exact place. Our beds had to be perfect: tight corners and covers as smooth as ice. The instructor would bounce a quarter off of the bed, and if it didn't jump back up at him, the consequences would be rough. I failed the quarter test only once. I spent all night scrubbing latrines with a toothbrush. That was the last time I ever had a problem with my bunk and locker inspection.

My unit was made up of young men from all over the United States. Each guy was from a different part of the country, and we each had our own story. But we also had something in common: We believed the group was more important than any one person. We were willing to sacrifice our individuality for the good of the unit. I had never before experienced that type of bond, and it was powerful. We began to gel, to work together as one. We were small parts in a giant machine that would soon unleash its fury far from home.

Early in my training, I had taken an assessment to see which military occupational specialty (MOS) I qualified for. After Basic Training, the soldiers in our unit went off to their AIT, or Advanced Individualized Training. Mine was for (153a), or Warrant Officer training, at the Hanchey Army Heliport at Fort Rucker, Alabama. I had qualified for and selected rotary wing aviation. I wanted to fly helicopters. I can't say that there was some deep-seated desire to fly; but the combination of freedom and power appealed to me, and when I learned that I would be delivering troops and rescuing the wounded in the field, that settled it. I could do something exciting while helping my guys.

Letter #5

2/16/72
Camp Radcliffe
An Khe Vietnam

A few days before my thirteenth birthday, my father came to talk to me. I was expecting it. He told me that I was to go off into the forest on my own. It was tribal tradition; every boy had to prove himself by spending three nights alone in the woods. It was called yitcarese, or "the transformation."

"You may not take anything but the clothes on your back," my father said. "You must survive on your own, with only your ability and knowledge of the land to guide you.

"But you won't be alone," he continued. "During this time, your ip-sah-keen, or spirit animal, will appear. You must pay close attention; it will come at an unexpected moment. It can help you return safely, but only if you can interpret its message.

61

"I will walk you into the mountains and from there you will con-
tinue on, alone. You will spend three nights. When you return, you
will not speak of what happened. That is between you and your ip-sah-
keen. Even if it takes longer than three nights, do not return home
without having known your ip-sah-keen. There are stories of young
men who returned having never met their ip-sah-keen. Their lives were
empty and without meaning or purpose."

Without accomplishing yitcarese, my father told me, I could never
grow up. I would never become a man. My father was a pretty direct
person.

I didn't feel prepared. I was scared. Were these feelings normal? I
couldn't talk to anyone about it. It was against tradition to discuss
one's yitcarese, so I couldn't seek advice from anybody, or even bring it
up in conversation. Once in a while I'd hear some of the older boys and
young men talk about it, but only in generalities, sharing obvious ad-
vice, like, "Always keep your eyes open," or, "Find a safe spot where
you can rest," but their words didn't hold any emotion. Did the other
kids feel similar to me before their journey? I couldn't know.

"That's it?" I asked Desiree.

"That's all there is," she said.

"But we don't know what happened," I said.

"Yeah, we do," she answered. "Sometime after the last letter
was sent, Warrant Officer Franklin Summers was KIA."

"What's KIA?"

"Killed in action," she said, her light beam scanning the area
around the tree clock. "Helicopters rely on speed and maneu-
verability. A pilot would take off from base and fly low over the
jungle top to avoid detection. He'd bring it down in a pre-

designated area called an *LZ*, or landing zone. LZ's are where the helos are most vulnerable to enemy fire. For a few seconds, the chopper is a sitting duck while troops are being offloaded and the injured put on board. Being a helicopter pilot in Vietnam required bravery, skill, and quick reflexes. And some luck."

"So how do you think he died?" I asked.

"I don't know," she responded. "We could probably research and find out, but I haven't."

"You know a lot about helicopters," I said. "And Vietnam."

"Yeah, I like to read," she said. "There's a lot of time for that at Mama's. Now we need to make this area look like it did when we got here, just in case." *Just in case.*

Desiree put the letters back inside the metal container, replaced the top, and stuck it back into the hole. We grabbed the dirt clump by the handles, walked it over, and placed it carefully into the space it had occupied. She took the shovel and spread out some dirt around the perimeter of the clump, trying to make it look undisturbed. One of the dirt clumps had fallen on the way back to the hole; she crushed it with her foot and kicked the remaining smaller chunks away.

We adjusted our headlamps, checked the place one more time for anything we might have left behind, and began the trip back to Mama's, Desiree in front. Acer materialized out of the brush, panting heavily. I turned to look back at the strange tree formation one last time.

The hike back went by in a dark blur. I was lost in the letters. They had given me a new perspective on Frank. He had been waiting for his father to come back from the war so he could find his ip-sah-keen and complete his yitcarese, so he could become a man. But his father never came back. In Frank's mind, his life could never be complete. It really couldn't even start.

The death of Warrant Officer Franklin Summers had left a hole inside of Frank, and to fill it he had buried the last words his dad had ever written to him inside a model train box under two feet of dirt. And along with those words, he had buried anger. Lots of it.

Chapter XII: The Garden

When I got to breakfast the next morning, only Frank and Mama were at the table. "Frank," said Mama, "today you're taking Danny on your perimeter walk."

"Yeah, I know," he said, already aggravated. He turned to me. "We'll leave this afternoon, 1300 hours." I did the math. One o'clock. "I move fast. You better keep up."

"Don't worry about me," I countered, brimming with fake confidence. Frank ignored my reply, instead focusing his energy on re-stacking and aligning his pile of pancakes.

"So, Danny," Mama said, "there's been a change of plans. Frank is going to bring you back up through the valley, to your place. The route runs parallel to the river for the most part, but well inland from it. If your mom has returned, you'll stay. I would appreciate letting Frank spend the night. The next morning, he can hike back down here. In case she's not there, you guys will head back here."

"Why can't we stay at my house if my mom's not there?" I asked Mama.

"We have to assume that the big guy is still running around the woods," she said. "And your house being dark, without power, well, that's just not safe. Honestly, we don't know what is happening up there. Frank will bring a gun. I pray he won't have to use it."

The thought of spending the night with Frank sent a shiver up my spine, almost made me queasy. I had a weird feeling that he had something in store for me, something I couldn't prepare for. The only other time I had been alone with him, he had been pressing a gun against my back. Around Mama, Frank begrudg-ingly followed her instructions; away from her, I didn't know.

"Danny," Mama continued, "you have a couple hours before you leave. Might as well be productive. Why don't you find your composting partner down in the garden and she'll put you to work."

I left the table and went out to find Desiree. From the bottom of the stairs, Acer looked up and noticed me, but only climbed two steps before changing his mind, stretching his front legs, and lying down. I patted him on the head as I passed him on my way to the garden.

"Desiree?" I called out.

"I'm down here."

I walked around to the back of the shed and found her work-ing, watering a flat tray of what looked like just plain dirt.

"Is there anything in there?" I asked.

"Just because you can't see something doesn't mean it doesn't exist," she said. "If you don't water the flat, the seeds will never germinate. A lot goes on beneath the surface."

"Mama sent me down to compost," I told her. "Can you help get me started?" We walked down to the composting area. There were three large piles, some buckets, and garden tools.

"You're probably not going to be here at Mama's long, so I won't bore you with the entire chemical process. But basically, we are putting green and brown together. Nitrogen is the green, in the form of vegetable peelings, grass cuttings, coffee grounds, whatever. The brown is the carbon: mostly leaves, but also egg shells, newspaper, cardboard. Once we combine the materials, they begin to breakdown, or decompose. The microbes need oxygen to do their work, so the pile needs to be turned over. That's where you come in. You're going to turn the compost today."

"Doesn't sound too difficult," I said.

"It's actually much more precise than I described it," she said. "A lot can go wrong. But the job I'm giving you, you can't screw it up."

"Thanks for the vote of confidence," I said.

"Did you just make a joke?" she asked, pushing a shovel hard into my hands. I moved back a step.

"Yeah," I said. "It was. It was - a joke." I practically swallowed the words.

"It wasn't funny."

She stared at me blankly. Was she really upset? Why? I couldn't think of anything to say. I felt my face getting red.

"Danny."

"What?"

"I'm messing with you."

"Of course. I knew that." I didn't know that. But I could breathe again. Being around Desiree was doing something to me. I wasn't sure what, but every time I was near her, I feltsomething. I'm not sure there's a word to describe it. Maybe just that. I felt.

"Go back up to the shed," she told me, "and switch this shovel out for the flathead. On the way back down, you'll see a black bucket next to the tables that hold the flats. Bring it too."

I trudged back up the trail. On the ground in front of the shed there were two rolled-up sleeping bags and a lantern. A large metal-frame backpack leaned against the shed, next to a coiled-up rope. Frank was standing in the doorway to the shed, his wide body completely blocking it.

"What do *you* want?" he asked me. The revulsion in his voice was palpable.

"I need a flathead shovel," I said. "I'm going to turn the compost." Sounded important enough.

He ignored me. I stood there for a second, unsure of what to do. Then, I stepped past him and into the shed, expecting to feel his shoulder knock me off balance. Instead, he turned away from me and toward the counter. There was a disassembled weapon there, a pistol. The parts were laid out on a greasy towel, spaced uniformly from each other. It looked like a museum display. Frank was holding a part of the gun I didn't recognize, wiping it down with a rag. I grabbed the shovel from the corner and left the shed, picking up the black bucket on my way back down.

Turning the compost was hard work, but it felt good to move, to sweat. It was hot out, and there was no shade. Every few minutes I stopped to drink water out of the hose.

For the first time since my fall back at the woodpile, it felt like my mind cleared. I wondered if my mom had returned home. She had planned to be gone for two days, and it had been three already. What would she think, how would she feel, when she discovered I wasn't there, that there was no power, and that her bedroom window had been smashed out?

Chapter XIII: Desiree's Room

It was almost time to head out with Frank. I was washing up in the mudroom, changing into some clothes that Mama had given me because what I had worn to compost was too dirty and smelly to wear on the hike. Acer was curled up in the mudroom shower, his head resting on the tile ledge, looking up at me pathetically. He sensed I was leaving.

Then, a quiet knock at the door. I thought it came from the kitchen-side door, but when I opened it, no one was there. I turned around to see a black boot was sticking through the doggy door.

"Hey!" came a loud whisper.

"What?" I whispered back.

The boot disappeared from Acer's entryway, replaced by an index finger beckoning me down to its level.

"Come down here."

I got down on all fours. Desiree pulled back on the doggy door's black rubber flap and her face appeared. Maybe it was the light or that I had not paid enough attention before but she had these little red flecks in the pupils of her eyes, tiny twinkling stars against a brown sky.

"Frank's still packing supplies," she said. "Meet me in my room. I may not see you again, and I want to say goodbye." The flap dropped and smacked me in the face. *May not see you again?*

I finished changing. I didn't know what to do with the old, smelly clothes, so I balled them up and left them in the corner of the mudroom. I wasn't sure how Frank would react if he found out I was in Desiree's room, but I figured he was already going to make the hike a living hell for me, so what did I have to lose? Plus, Desiree was only Frank's girlfriend in his own mind.

I went out to the living room. Through the sliding glass door, I could see Frank down by the shed. I walked down the hallway to Desiree's room and almost knocked, but then didn't.

"You in there?" I asked.

"Come in," she said. "Close the door behind you."

The room was in no better shape than when I had peeked in the other night. The plant was still tipped over, the bed covers on the floor. The writing on the wall was in thick, permanent marker.

Desiree was sitting at the foot of the bed. Her hair was pulled back in a tight ponytail, except for one thick strand that fell in front of her face. She didn't look up. In her hand was a small notebook, maybe a stenographer's pad, which she closed when she saw me look at it. I stood there for a second, looking around, not knowing what to say. Awkward. She had invited me in but was in no hurry to start a conversation.

"Can I read your poem?" I asked her, pointing to the wall.

"It's a free country," she said, turning to look at her poem. "That was one of my early ones, when I first moved to Mama's place. Before I started using the notebooks. Not very good."

I read it to myself while she looked through her notebook.

wispy cloud
if I move my head back and forth
i can see it
but I don't
just pretend it isn't there

a cold breeze
they can't feel
For them just sunshine
abundant heat and warmth

the sky darkens
distant thunder
rain
lightening
scaring me
soaking me

i crawl inside
get smaller and smaller
but
i'm still here
always here

"It's a poem about the weather," I said.

"Yep." She was writing in her pad and didn't look up.

"But it's not really about the weather."

"Nope." She sat up, pulled the chair out from under her desk, opened the drawer, and took out a pack of black markers.

"Do these storms come often?" I knew it was a personal question, but I asked anyway.

"Can't predict them," she said. "No forecast models." She gestured to the chair. I sat, my arm resting on the desk, next to the tipped-over plant.

"When a storm approaches," she said, "you can feel it coming. But there's nothing you can do. You can't avoid it. There's no shelter from it. It's just - pure alone."

She looked at me as if she was asking if I could understand. I couldn't, not really. The sun through her window found the red specks in her eyes again. I wondered what she saw in mine. Was there anything to see in them?

Desiree pulled a marker from the pack, uncapped it, and faced the wall, her knees digging into the mattress. Starting from the last word and moving backward, she began to cross out her poem, right to left, up toward the top, until a thick black line ran through each line, every word. She wasn't deleting the poem; the words could still be read. But the power of the poem had been depleted, drained, and the words no longer held meaning. A disposable, single-use poem.

"Isn't there someone you can talk to?" I asked her. "Some kind of medicine you can take?"

"I'm here because my parents wanted to force me to take meds," Desiree said. "I wouldn't do it. And I won't do it. I don't want chemicals messing with my brain's natural function."

"And Mama doesn't insist you take them?" I asked.

"Yeah, she does," Desiree said, "but I cheek 'em."

I was about to ask what that meant but then it came to me. Mama gave her medication in those little paper cups, like the one I had seen at dinner. Desiree pretended to swallow the

73

pills, but instead hid them in her cheek, and then spit them out after she left the table.

I looked down. I had been absent-mindedly drawing designs in the spilled plant dirt with my finger, using the desk as a canvas. There were two parallel, straight lines, about six inches apart. In between the lines I had made ten marks. Each had five points to them, like little hands. It was weird. I had never seen anything like it before. I didn't know why I would do it.

Chapter XIV: Security Patrol

Frank was hunched over on one knee, his back to me. He had on army fatigues, green, brown and tan splotches swirled in random patterns. His pants were pressed flat, with a just-ironed look, and his sleeves were evenly rolled up to his biceps. The boots were polished, black and shiny. A camouflage wide-brim hat was pulled low over his forehead, long, dark hair spilling out.

Without turning around, he handed me one canteen. As I was thinking about how best to carry it, he thrust the other canteen into my hand. I put the straps over my head and pulled them over opposite shoulders so that they crossed at my chest. They were heavier than they looked. He tossed the tent bag over his shoulder, in my general direction, and I caught it. The metal poles shifted awkwardly inside the canvas.

Frank directed a grunt toward a backpack that had a sleeping bag strapped to the bottom of it. His way of telling me that he expected me to wear it. I unzipped the backpack and took a quick peek inside: sandwiches, chips, fruit, granola bars, something rectangular wrapped in a large plastic baggie packed inside crushed ice. I pulled the backpack over my shoulders. It was heavy but the fit was good.

I walked a few yards back and forth, testing my balance. The canteens bounced against my hips. It wasn't too difficult to adjust to the shifting weight of the gear, but I had to be twenty-five pounds heavier with it on.

Frank pulled on a larger pack, a rolled-up sleeping bag tied to the top. It looked heavy, but his muscles seemed to welcome the strain. He held a shovel in his left hand. It looked like the same one Desiree and I had taken to the tree clock. Finally, after cleaning, oiling and reassembling the pistol, he was taking it with him. It was holstered on his right hip, a leather strap snapped over the handle. I hoped the safety was on.

There was no heads-up that we were leaving; he just took off, up the same wide dirt path that Desiree and I had taken the night before. Frank's legs didn't seem to be moving very fast, but he walked quickly; I struggled to keep up. By the time I passed the stacked firewood, I was probably fifty feet in back of him.

The trail narrowed. The trees that lined both sides tilted inward, creating a tunnel effect. The light was less intense and the temperature cooler. It didn't look familiar, and my instincts told me that we weren't heading toward my house, or, if we were, it was a different route. I tried not to think about where we were going, and instead, focused on the military precision of Frank's steps, both as a way of keeping up with him as well as taking my mind off the weight I was carrying.

I increased my pace to a jog for a minute and caught up to him, hanging about ten feet back to give him space and keep a safe distance. He didn't seem to be in the mood to have a conversation. But then, he never was. It would be a lonely feeling never to talk to someone unless you have to.

Just as I felt like I had found a rhythm along the mostly flat path, we took a sudden left turn and the terrain became steeper. The trail wasn't as wide. After maybe fifteen yards, the trail turned back to the right. We continued to climb. Left. Climb. Right. Climb. Left. Climb. With each switchback we took, the backpack got heavier.

Then, after navigating between two boulders that stuck out of the dirt at awkward angles, we were out of the switchbacks. I turned to look back down at the zigzagging trail behind us. We had probably gained two hundred feet in elevation.

Frank stopped, so I did, too. He was still and quiet. I looked around, but nothing stood out as unusual. I couldn't make out a trail ahead, just land sloping at a gentle rise and severely left to right. It was barren except for some long, brown grass-like weeds.

"This is called 'the meadow'," Frank said. His words surprised me; not the actual words, but the fact that he was speaking to me. I had only ever heard him angry. It seemed like he was forcing himself to have a normal conversation.

"We'll eat here," he said, turning around to face me and making fleeting eye contact. "There's still a big hike ahead of us."

"Are we heading to my place?" I asked him, bracing for a sarcastic response.

"We're still on perimeter patrol," Frank said. "After we loop around the property, we'll head up to your mom's house. But, instead of following the river, we'll take a longer route that will bring us up to your property from behind." I wondered how Frank could know exactly where I lived. But I figured that he had become familiar with the whole area through these long hikes.

The water tasted better than good. They say water has no taste, but I disagree. Frank handed me a sandwich and an apple from his pack. We sat on top of the boulders, a view of the slanted terrain we would tackle next laid out in front of us. Two willow trees provided dappled shade from the late afternoon sun. It was quiet for a couple minutes while we ate. If I closed my eyes, I could almost imagine that we were just two friends enjoying lunch out in nature. Then Frank spoke.

"You ever wonder who used to live here?" His question caught me off guard. He had never asked me my opinion about anything. I couldn't imagine him caring.

"What do you mean?" I asked. "Are you talking about the early people of this area?"

Frank washed down the last of his sandwich with a swig from his canteen and wiped his mouth with a handkerchief that he pulled from his pocket. He folded it into a square, and then another smaller square, before carefully placing it back into the pocket.

"You know," he replied, "people lived around here peacefully for thousands of years. And they would have continued to live here."

"Would have?"

"Yes," Frank replied softly, removing his hat. "Would have." He stared ahead toward the open space in front of us, a vacant, far-off look in his eyes. "But then, the Others came. They came and they destroyed everything."

The Others. Frank's dad had mentioned them in one of the letters. *The Others tried to give us a name because of how we looked, but we did not accept it. The Others pushed their culture and traditions on us. We did not accept them.*

"The Others?"

"Who do you think you're more like, Danny?" Frank asked, ignoring my question. "The Original People, or the Others?" There was an edge to his voice now, a false curiosity that failed to mask anger.

"I don't know much about the Original People," I answered. "And I don't think I have any native blood in me. So, I guess I'd be more like…the Others."

"We need to move," Frank said. "Gear up." I stood and began to strap on my gear. I wasn't sure why, but I was relieved that the conversation was over. Frank started up the slanted grade and hit full stride quickly, as I struggled to keep up. The pack felt heavier and my feet felt slower than when we were snaking up the trail just a few minutes before. The combination of trying to keep leaning left to avoid falling to the right, and the heat, and the pack, was taking its toll. I fell behind.

We were walking toward what looked like a fence stuck between two rocks. Frank reached the top of the slanted grade before I did and continued walking just as easily as if he were on flat ground like he had some internal motor that automatically switched on when it was needed.

The "fence" I had seen from the bottom of the grade was actually jagged rocks sticking out toward each other, like two hands with fingers pointing in random directions, some almost but not quite touching. Not a place you'd want to run through, unless your goal was to rip skin off your body. There was just enough room between the rocks to squeeze through, after we took off our packs and turned sideways.

We emerged into a completely different environment. A canopy of trees blocked out the sun, creating thin, strong columns of light that beamed down between the leaves, crossing each other in a million shining intersections. The air was cooler. The trail was thinner than before, but more defined. And it was flat, which I desperately needed.

A sheer granite wall to my left wrapped around the face of the mountain until it disappeared above me. Hearty patches of yellowish-brown scrub brush poked out from crooked crevices. To my right was a sheer drop of maybe two hundred feet.

Frank slowed for a moment, then resumed his robotic pace. The trail narrowed again. It was now only about a foot wider than Frank. Jagged rocks pockmarked the dirt. I picked one up and tossed it over the edge. I listened for it to land but heard nothing. Bull Run River was cutting through the valley below, its roar liquid silence at our altitude.

"This part of the terrain is called 'moonscape'," Frank said, his back to me. It was an accurate title. Dry, dusty and sparse, it had a desolate, lunar look. I wondered who had named it "moonscape" -was the name something that only Frank used?

I had been lost in thought and didn't realize that we were walking downhill. Using different muscles was a relief on my legs, but a temporary one. The next rise never seemed very far off. The thought that I had no idea where I was entered my mind, but again, I calmed myself with the theory that Mama would not let anything happen to me while she knew Frank was with me. Except Mama was miles away.

The trail meandered, left and right, each segment maybe forty feet long before turning the other way. It was the easiest part of our trek so far, the pattern of gentle turns allowing me to conserve some energy.

"Roller coaster," Frank barked back at me, adjusting the straps on his pack and wiping his brow with the perfectly folded handkerchief. As if obeying his observation, the trail quickly rose twenty feet in elevation, peaked, and then fell, rose and fell, snaking left and then right again. So much for conserving energy.

It was during this portion of our perimeter hike, late in the day when the shadows from the trees that lined the "roller coaster" were the longest of the afternoon, that Frank suggested another stop. Actually, it wasn't a suggestion. He never suggested anything. He just stopped, pulled off his pack, removed his canteen, and sat. I did the same.

We were at the top of a rise. I had been so occupied with keeping up with Frank, who was much stronger than I was and a far superior hiker, that I hadn't been looking around to see if I could recognize anything or use any clues from the terrain to determine my position relative to my property. I was beyond lost, totally dependent on Frank.

"I want to show you something," Frank said. He dug into the front left pocket of his camouflage pants and pulled out a folded, wrinkled and very faded brown piece of paper, about the color of a grocery bag, and painstakingly unfolded it. Then he leaned in next to me, like he was about to tell me a secret.

"Warrant Officer gave me this," he said. "It's a map of the entire area." Was that pride in his voice? I wasn't sure. "The whole valley. You can see both rivers here," he said, pointing to two faded but thick light blue lines. The map didn't look like a map, at least not to me. It was a hazy swirl of mixed up colors, with jagged shapes and different sized arrows pointing in seemingly random directions. I couldn't make out anything besides the rivers.

"This is the perimeter we're walking, right here," he continued, running his index finger about midway up the left edge of the map. "Here's Mama's place, at the very south end. Here's where I captured you. And then, up here at the north end of the valley, is your property."

I was uncomfortable with Frank being so close to me. But I also felt something else, something I didn't expect to feel: privilege. I was part of his exclusive club, at least right that second; Frank trusted me enough to show me the map.

"Where exactly are we on this?" I asked him.

"At this scale, there are only a few specific locations that the map indicates," Frank replied, his big hand hovering over the map, fingers spread wide. "We're looking at a valley that's roughly 14 miles by 6 miles. That's over 50,000 acres. Hard to put any detail in, but you can notice a few things. The valley. The rivers. But the most important thing around here, you don't need a *map* to see."

"And what's that?"

Frank's eyes moved slowly off the map and up to me. He lifted his arm and pointed past me, off to his right. I turned to look. Past a vast expanse of undulating forest, maybe a mile away, a rock jutted out from the valley floor.

"What, the rock?"

"What do you notice about it?" he asked me. I wasn't sure where he was going with this. What would I notice about a rock?

"The elevation?" I guessed weakly, not wanting to appear too clueless.

"No," he shot back. "What else?"

I looked again. The rock emerged, roughly pyramid-shaped, from a relatively flat layer of trees. The top was flat, except for a wide crack on the left side that had created a wide crevasse that, if you turned your head sideways, looked almost like a mouth. The most noticeable feature was a sharp granite spire that protruded out vertically from the base maybe twenty feet into the air, its stark gray a contrast to the fading light of the pale blue sky behind it. If the crevasse was a mouth, then the spire was a nose.

A nose.

The Witch's Nose.

The air left my lungs evenly, like a balloon with a silent, slow leak. I was paralyzed, staring at the sharp rock column. How could Frank know I knew about the Witch's Nose?

"You're wondering how I know that you know," Frank said, reading my mind. The idea of lying to him, fabricating some complicated explanation, flashed through my mind. Look him in the eye and deny everything. But I didn't. I couldn't. I was caught. I knew it. And Frank knew it.

"It's true," he said, folding up the map even more carefully than he had unfolded it. What was true? That the rock was the Witch's Nose?

Then it really hit me. He knew. *He knew.* That I went into the woods with Desiree. That we dug up the train box. That we read the letters. He knew everything, and I was stuck out here in the woods with him.

"It's true." I didn't want to know what was true.

"What's true?" I half-croaked.

"What Desiree said to you, back at Mama's place," he continued. "I *am* a deep sleeper. But only *after* I fall asleep." Gone was the strained attempt at normal conversation. Back was the Frank I knew: the icy cold words, the dead-eyed stare.

"What are you talking about?"

It was a delay tactic, a futile pump on the brakes, trying and stop the conversation from going where I knew it was going. He stood up, re-tucked his shirt, and pulled on his pack.

"Get up, kal-san-gip," Frank ordered me, repeating the strange word he had called me during our first encounter in the forest, three days ago. "Get your crap. We're leaving. You're going to do something."

I got up but I didn't put on my gear. I thought about running. With nothing. Into nowhere. But of course, I didn't. I just stood there, arms at my side, like an idiot.

"Are you deaf, boy?" Frank screamed at me, stepping closer. He was expanding as he moved into my airspace, growing wider and taller with each inch of my space that he was invading. His face was burgundy red. Thick veins popped from his forearms. I stumbled back.

"Either you put on that pack or I put it on for you!" he yelled.

I put on the pack. He turned around and took a couple steps down the trail before stopping again and turning around to face me. For the first time in a while, I noticed the gun on his hip.

"Since you've already read the letters," Frank said, "I'm going to show you something you haven't seen. It's the missing piece of the puzzle. Let's go." A rustling in the trees above us became a dark cloud of birds that splintered into a thousand directions, dissipating into the sky.

He walked and I followed, far enough behind so I could try to elude the funnel of hatred emanating from him. The Witch's Nose was visible on my right. Frank's father had used it to orient himself to stay safe. I wondered if I was on the safe side.

Frank turned and took a trail that branched off to the left, similar to one of the switchbacks but in a different direction. He was walking faster now. My legs were burning again, and an area on the left side of my lower back was irritated and painful. One of the screws that held the frame of the backpack together was rubbing against my skin, next to my spine. Holding my hand between the screw and my back while I walked was awkward but relieved the pain.

The Witch's Nose followed me in my peripheral vision before dipping below a grove of pines. We hiked for another half hour or so, the elevation dropping and the signs of a trail disappearing, becoming miniature streams that snaked through leaves and mud.

Then, without warning, I felt like collapsing. We were hiking the bottom of a narrow canyon, when all of my energy just disappeared. Although I had been unaware of it, the long trek had been gradually sapping me of my strength. I had been pushing on through adrenaline only. Now, like a battery that had reached the end of its life cycle, I was done. I stopped, bent over, hands on my knees. Frank was going to love this.

"What's wrong?!" He bellowed back angrily, his arms stretched wide like he couldn't believe what he was seeing.

"I need a minute," I gasped. "Water. And to sit." I began to unwrap one of the canteen straps.

"No!" he roared, walking back to me. "We're too close to stop! Just up there!" He pointed. I looked. A thin, crooked trail

85

wrapped around the side of a grassy hill and then disappeared. Frank pulled a canteen strap off my shoulder, uncapped it, and lifted it. Water cascaded over my head and down my back. I'm not sure what the desired effect was (punishment?), but it woke me up and gave me enough energy to continue.

Then, somehow, I had made it. We were there. The Witch's Nose. I collapsed against the cool granite surface and peeled off my backpack. I was soaking wet. My legs and shoulders throbbed.

Frank was unpacking, methodically removing and placing his gear along a flat rock ledge behind him. We were either going to stay up on the rock overnight, or he wanted to examine all his items and then repack. Either way, it looked like we would be here for a while. I was relieved. The hike had completely drained me. But there was some anxiety, too; Frank had said he wanted me to "do something," and I doubted that something was just making the final push to the Witch's Nose. It couldn't be that easy.

Frank unrolled his sleeping bag, doubling it over width-wise. I struggled to my feet and did the same to mine. He unhooked the lantern and put it down on the ledge, next to the gun. Then, from his backpack he pulled out a plastic bag that dripped water. He put it down, stood, and began to gather kindling from the perimeter of the rock's face.

Frank's back was to me. I had a good view of the gun, its clean, machine-shopped metal leaning incongruously against an outcropping of granite. I was closer to it than Frank. I could grab it before Frank even realized what had happened. I'd never held a weapon, let alone aimed or fired one. Frank would know that. He would know that I'd be bluffing. But even if he believed I knew how to use one, what then? I didn't know where I was, and I couldn't force him to lead me out of the forest because my only threat would be to shoot him, and if I did that, I'd be on my own, and still lost.

I snapped back to reality to see Frank hunched over at the edge of the rock, building a bed of small sticks and twigs. The kindling was uniform in size, six inches long and half an inch around. The sticks formed as perfect of a cube as could be made, about 6 x 6 x 6 inches. He filled the space inside the cube with shredded paper he pulled out from one of his many pockets.

"Look in your backpack," he told me. "Pull out the folded metal frame."

Neither of us had said anything for a while, and his words, although flat and cold, filled the void. I searched for the thing he was talking about. Before I had completely removed it from my pack, Frank was next to me, snatching it from my hands. He stared coldly at me while unfolding its four metal legs. Next, he pulled out a book of matches, ripped off two of them, and lit the crumbled-up paper on fire in a couple different places. It caught quickly and began to burn. He placed the metal structure over the fire.

Then he unwrapped the large, square steak that he had kept cold during our hike. I'm not sure what cut it was, or even from what kind of animal, but it looked lean. He placed the meat on the grill. It sizzled and popped, the sound mixing with the buzz of the early evening cicadas. The smell made my mouth water. A fork appeared in Frank's hand and he used it to turn the meat over.

After a few minutes, Frank used a pocketknife to cut the steak into two equal-sized rectangles. Hungry and anxious is a weird combination, but that's what I was feeling.

Steam rose from the piece he handed me. I grabbed it between index finger and thumb. My fingers began to burn. Had Frank not been there, I would have dropped it immediately. But I held my piece, not wanting to look like a wimp, and it took an impossibly long time to cool off before I could take a bite. Frank took his dinner around the other side of the Nose, the one section of the rock I hadn't yet seen. I sat and ate my food and gave Frank a little space and time before walking over to join him.

He was standing over a hole that appeared to be cut directly out of the rock. I approached it and peered in. It had no visible bottom, but my side of the pit had a rope ladder bolted to the side and extending down, I didn't know how far. I looked up at Frank. He had something in his hand.

"Sit down," he commanded. "You know, the way you and my girlfriend did at Tree Circle, with your legs in the hole."

I sat, my legs dangling into the darkness. I knew Frank had followed me and Desiree into the woods, but the thought of him watching us digging up the metal box, listening to Desiree read the letters...it just made me sick. The taste of steak in my mouth turned to puke.

"Do you know what these are?" he asked, holding up some folded pieces of paper.

"Pieces of paper?"

"Yes, pieces of paper, smart-ass kap-seese," he replied, his eyes narrowing with a smirk. "Do you know what's written on them?"

"No, I don't," I said.

"Take a wild guess," Frank responded. "First thing that comes to your mind."

"A letter?"

"Wow, are you psychic?" he asked sarcastically. "Yes, it's a letter." He unfolded it and, maybe not knowing he was doing it, pressed the papers against his chest. "From Warrant Officer. The sixth letter. The last letter." He extended the letter out to me. I hesitated, then took it.

"Go ahead," he told me. "Read it out loud."

"It's none of my business," I said, reaching over the hole, trying in vain to hand the letter back to him.

"That didn't stop you before."

Frank stood, dusted off his pants, and re-tucked his shirt. Then he turned and walked a few feet to the edge of the rock. He stood there, looking out over the quickly darkening woods. I sat, holding his letter, wishing I was anywhere else in the world.

At the time, back in the woods with Desiree, it had seemed so exciting, a victimless crime. But the truth was that Desiree and I had violated Frank's privacy. Without his permission, we had peered through a window at the most intimate of communication between a father and his son. We had done it, and it couldn't be undone. I felt ashamed.

And now he was insisting that I read the letter out loud. I had no choice. I had to. Maybe, in some small way, it would lighten the guilt I felt.

Chapter XV: Yitcarese

Letter #6

4/5/72
Camp Radcliffe
An Khe Vietnam

Throughout my life I was careful to listen to my father and respect the traditions of our tribe. But there are other important things on this earth, as important as our customs. Like the bond that men share when they depend on each other. Like the way honesty links a man and his son. I cannot keep from you something that I would have wanted my father to share with me. That's why, although it breaks tradition, I am going to tell you about my yitcarese.

You have a choice. If tribal tradition runs so strong in your blood that you cannot in good conscience listen to my journey, stop reading now. I will respect your decision. I will not be upset.

I stopped reading and looked at Frank. Did he want me to continue? A simple nod answered my question.

For the middle of summer, the day of my yitcarese was unseasonably cold. I knew no one would come by to wish me good luck. No one did. I waited for my father to come for me. He arrived in silence. Not unusual. I could read nothing on his face that said this day was different than any other. He motioned for me to follow. We walked out of the village along the main trail. I saw no one along the route, save the fleeting image of a little boy peeking out from behind a small square window in the final cabin we passed.

I wore patched-up blue jeans and basic leather sandals, and a tie-dyed t-shirt underneath a thin leather vest. The shirt had appeared on my bed two days before. It had an intricate pattern of muted black and brown splotches that orbited a fractured explosion of bright reds, oranges and yellows. I didn't know who had made it, or why he or she had given it me, and there was no one to ask. I wanted to imagine it would bring me good luck and strength.

The cold temperature and my anxiety conspired to produce a strong shiver in my body. I stayed a few feet behind my father, hoping he wouldn't interpret it as fear - although that's exactly what it was. We walked silently, separated by unspoken rules. We might have hiked for two hours. It could have been twice that, maybe less; I wasn't sure.

He stopped. I did too. I looked around. Nothing familiar and I could no longer see the Witch's Nose. I don't know what my father was thinking at that moment, but it may have been something like, "Don't mess this up." Then, he turned around and walked away. I was alone.

What I had to do sounded simple enough. Find food and drink. Stay warm. Locate my ip-sah-keen. Get home. Four steps.

I could identify some edible plants and mushrooms, so finding food wasn't my highest priority. And, with the recent storms, rain runoff was plentiful, so I would be able to find water. My biggest challenge would be staying warm. Temperatures could drop into the 30s at night, and sometimes colder when the sky was clear, when there were no clouds to act as a barrier to prevent the warm air from rising.

I had never perfected the art of starting a fire through friction, by rubbing two sticks together. I couldn't seem to generate the speed, the rapid back-and-forth spin with my hands that would create sufficient heat for the spark. I had resigned myself to the fact that I wouldn't be sitting next to a warm fire for the next few nights, so finding good shelter, a place that might hold some residual heat from the day, would be crucial. I was thinking some sort of cave or cavern. Worst-case scenario, I could always cover myself with leaves and spend the night shivering, but not freezing.

Early afternoon. The woods seemed to have anticipated my arrival and had fallen silent, hidden eyes watching me. From my peripheral vision a flash of movement caught my eye. I looked but it was gone. Then, from behind some trees, low to the ground, something was moving in the direction of a rock outcropping about forty feet away. My first thought was bobcat. It was too fast to have been anything larger.

I forgot about it and started looking around for anything useful I could find. I stumbled upon a bowl-shaped piece of tree bark that would work for collecting edible flowers and mushrooms. With a few hours of daylight remaining, I went about scouring the area for food.

Fennel was plentiful and I pulled enough off to nearly fill my basket. Nearby was a patch of clover. The white, puffy flower heads could be eaten raw, but didn't taste great. The stems had a slightly better flavor, but I had known since I had been little that too many of them could cause stomach pain. I pulled off a bunch of the clover. A couple hundred yards away, a stream provided me a fresh drink of clear, cold water.

I had been wandering for a while, looking for shelter, feeling pretty confident. My good start had me relaxed for the first time in a couple days. The thought that I wasn't stressed out contributed to my sense of well-being. There was something liberating about being alone in the woods. I filled my lungs with fresh air. Maybe this was going to turn out all right, after all.

Then that was over. I sensed the blur again. It was in back of me, partially obscured by some cascara trees. I felt the ground move. My initial thought was earthquake, but the little red berries on the trees in front of me weren't shaking. I heard a sound, deep and low, almost guttural, a vibration from beneath me that ran from my feet up through my legs and into my torso. I didn't see the animal but I knew it was there, sensed it.

The bark bowl crunched under my feet as I ran, staccato pops of snapping branches and crunching twigs already gaining on me. I couldn't outrun it, but I was going to try. My body was channeling fear into energy, recycling terror into speed. Either I was moving faster than I ever had before or the animal was not giving 100% effort, because I was still alive.

There it was again, the flash, up on a rock ledge that rose above the forest floor, twenty yards ahead. I could clearly see four stubby legs now. Its tail appeared to be too big for its small body, and its ears pointed up almost vertically and were rounded off at the top. It was mostly gray, with fur darker brown closer to its paws. It was a fox. I continued to run and it seemed to be trying to stay a safe but visible distance ahead of me. It sounds crazy, but I was almost convinced that it wanted me to follow it. Could the fox be my ip-sah-keen? Why a fox? What if it wasn't? I pushed the thoughts from my mind and ran. Ran until my quads burned, until I could barely breathe. Then I ran some more.

My pace settled into something between a sprint and a jog. I calmed down and began to regulate my breathing. My body relaxed. The terrain began to look a little familiar. I was sure I had seen the area before. I recognized the marshy flatlands. The sun strained through some juniper trees. I looked up, above the tree line.

I wasn't sure what I was looking at. It was the right height, and the right color, but the angles looked all wrong. But I knew it was the Witch's Nose.

My friends and I had never been on it. When I asked my father if we could go, he had told me no. No explanation was offered, and I asked no questions. My friends received a similar answer from their *fathers. It was something we didn't do, something we didn't talk about. Would I dare go against my father's wishes? Being chased by a bear certainly seemed like extraordinary circumstances.*

The path up the rock was a set of switchbacks that had been cut directly into the side of the massive rock. Cut by whom, I didn't know. But erosion, water and wind could not by themselves have created the pattern. The angles formed by the intersecting ridges were too precise. Some ancient people, long ago, had carved the path into the rock, with tools, strength, and patience I could not even imagine.

I scrambled up to the first switchback. The path was wide enough that, if I leaned toward the rock, I could sort of walk-jog along. I crisscrossed the remaining switchbacks and the altitude increased. The trail got wider. I could run again, but it was becoming more difficult as the grade got steeper. Twice, I met a dead end: an impassable, sheer rock wall face. Why would those who had carved the trail create dead ends? I backtracked and took an alternate route. Then, I was there. I was at the Witch's Nose.

None of my friends had ever been. I walked around to where I thought I would be facing the general direction of my village and looked across the green expanse of forest. I wondered what my father would be doing...pacing nervously, waiting for my return? I doubted it. Not his style. I continued along the outside of the Nose, until I was almost back at the point where I had emerged from the trail.

The fox was there, looking like a small stuffed animal, its tail darting side to side. It was looking at me, its piercing, greenish-yellow eyes locked on to mine. This couldn't have been the animal that had chased me. That had to have been a bear. That's when I looked down and saw the hole.

It was formed, or cut, into a circle, slightly oblong on one side, and about four feet across. A rope ladder, frayed with age and darkened from the sun's rays, was bolted to the edge. I stepped closer and looked down into the hole. The rope ladder vanished into pitch black. The dark below seemed to be sucking the surface light down into it. I didn't want to go in, but there was no doubt that the bear had my scent and would eventually find me up here. And when the animal arrived, I'd have no choice but to go down in the hole, and in a hurry. At least this way I could be more careful and deliberate.

I turned so that my body faced the ladder and stepped down onto the first rung. Just two thick old rusty bolts, driven deep into the rock, kept the ladder, and me, from tumbling into the abyss below. I stepped down again and tested the ladder, gently bouncing up and down on it. It felt sturdy; my weight didn't even budge it. By the third step down, I could grab the top rung. The ladder wasn't rope; at least, not the kind of rope I was familiar with. It was made of strips of some type of strong plant, twisted tightly together and tied off at both ends, where it connected to the sides. I don't recall where or when I learned it, but I remembered that type of connection point was called a "whipping." The rungs had a smooth, strong, permanent feel to them. The ladder had been there a long time, and many people had used it.

My worry diminished as I descended into the darkness. There was no way the bear could follow me down. The rungs in front of me were no longer visible, but the pattern was predictable enough: right hand and left foot down, left hand and right foot down, repeat.

My foot hit the bottom. I stood in a dusty cone of sunlight and looked up, maybe twenty-five feet below the opening. A tunnel extended in two directions, opposite each other. The air was warm, almost moist. The walls were covered with swirling hues of rust-brown colors. I ran my hand along the rock surface. It was smooth, but every few inches, a sharp point rose out.

I began to walk in the direction of my village, or at least that's where I imagined I was heading. Slow and deliberate steps, my hand following the gently undulating contours of the cave wall.

The light from behind me faded away. My hand was now a virtual guide dog, my only receptor of information, fingers reporting back to me what they were feeling – rough, soft, smooth. I turned and looked back at the last wisp of light from the entrance. Now would be the last opportunity to turn around and still be sure I could get back to the opening.

There was no transition. I was eclipsed by complete darkness. I put my hand in front of my face. Nothing. I had never been in pitch black. My most vital sense was useless. My hand sensed the tunnel begin to curve left. Then it seemed to straighten out. The wall was rough now, pockmarked and pitted with whatever force had formed and punctured it so many millions of years ago. I ran my hand up the side of the tunnel as far as it would go to see if I could reach the ceiling. I couldn't and had no idea how far up it was. The ground felt soft beneath my feet, like I was walking on a layer of fine dust.

The air was warmer and thicker than before. It wasn't hard to breathe, but there was a distinct pressure on my chest. Perhaps it was from the massive bulk of rock on top of me. Or maybe it was the weight of my father's expectations. I couldn't forget what I had gone into the woods to do. By running to the Witch's Nose, I had ignored my father and the tribal elders. But going inside the Witch's Nose was even worse. No one would know I was here.

The prospect of completing my yitcarese was fading fast. I felt pretty confident that the little gray fox I had followed was my ip-sah-keen, but was there supposed to be some connection between us? I hadn't felt it. Even if it was my ip-sah-keen, what good could come from finding it if I never emerged from the mountain?

Lost in thought, I continued feeling my way through the tunnel until I realized that I was no longer touching anything. The wall was not there. My hand had lost contact. Gone was my connection to the world above, the only sense I could use.

A bolt of fear coursed through me. I couldn't feel anything, hear anything, or see anything. A person knows he exists because his senses tell him so. He can see the sky, touch a tree, smell a rose. If you take away the senses, the person ceases to be. Inside the Witch's Nose, I was a shell, a body; down here, I had no life. Down here, I wasn't.

The mountain had lured me up its crooked path, opened itself, and I had been willingly consumed and digested by it. The mountain didn't care. I could sit down and never get up again. I could starve, run out of water, and die. My body could mummify, become part of the rock. The mountain didn't care. So I sat. How long, I don't know. Ten minutes. An hour. Five hours. I just sat.

But something inside of me, some little sliver of light, a spark, wouldn't let me give up. I wanted to see my family again. I wanted to complete my yitcarese. I wanted to live. And I couldn't do any of those things, down here, curled up in a ball, waiting to die. There was a chance, however small, that, if there was an alternate way out, I could find it.

I stood up and began to walk. I zigzagged, back and forth, each turn wider than the one before, in one direction and then the other, hands outstretched, feeling for rock, all the while moving forward, deeper into the Witch's Nose.

I felt nothing. No matter how far I went in any direction, my hand felt nothing. How was this possible? Could the tunnel have opened into some kind of chamber? Suddenly my hand struck rock directly in front of me. It was the end, or the beginning, of a wall. I could wrap my arms around it and feel both sides. The surfaces felt the same, both scarred and pitted, with some smoother, deeper channels. Which way to go? I tried to calculate which side might lead me to the village by mentally retracing my steps, but I was too turned around and confused for that.

Chapter XVI: Not Alone

For the past few minutes, my eyes had been playing tricks on me, painting swirls of light and color as if my brain, with no information to process, had become bored and decided to entertain itself by generating its own designs, jagged sunspots and shimmery floaters that you might see if you pressed and held your hands against your eyes.

That's what I thought was happening when I noticed the faintest yellow glow ahead of me. I closed my eyes to see if the glow remained. It didn't. I opened them and there it was. It was real. There was a light source down here. It was not a flickering light, like that of a fire. It was consistent, constant. I couldn't see the source of the light, but it illuminated the tunnel. The light was comforting, because I could see again, but scary as well, because I didn't know what I would find when I reached its source.

"Hello?" My tone certainly wouldn't scare anyone off if they were here. "Hello?" Nothing. I approached a bend in the tunnel, dragging my fingers along the wall behind me. The light became stronger.

It's hard to describe something you've never seen before. There's nothing to compare it to, so words don't work. Imagine you're visiting a distant planet whose sun generated colors you were completely unfamiliar with, an alien spectrum of light. You return to Earth and attempt to explain what you saw. Impossible, because you could only compare your new colors to those colors known to exist in our world. This is how I feel trying to describe what I found that day inside the Witch's Nose.

First off, and this will sound crazy: the light, the Source, was a solid. By solid, I mean it was contained, or contained itself, into one finite space, and at the same time lighting the tunnel for thirty feet in all directions. The Source was about the size of a small backpack but had no fixed form; its shape changed constantly. It folded and gyrated into it-

self, intermittently pulsing with strong bursts of light - a warm, translucent glow, twisting, turning in, out, around, bending, rotating.

It sat in a circular protrusion that looked to have been carved out of the rock itself. By "sat," I mean it occupied a space just above the rock bowl, but didn't actually touch the bottom, instead levitating, hovering, an inch or so above it.

Now Frank, I know what you must be thinking. That I had spent too much time down there inside the Witch's Nose, that the pressure, the dark, the exhaustion had gotten to me. That, maybe, I was hallucinating. Standing there I considered that possibility. But the stuff was real.

Scattered about the ground were shattered pottery bowls: big broken shards, some smaller ones, and a few that were the size of large splinters. One bowl was intact and undamaged. It was tipped over onto its side, three short and stubby legs protruding out from its round belly. Its color was a cobalt or black, hard to tell. I reached down and tipped the bowl back onto its legs.

It started.

I was sitting now and I was no longer alone. There were four people with me, two women and two men. They were sitting cross-legged in a semi-circle, surrounding and facing the light. I could not see their faces. They wore thin, plain tan-colored cloths that covered them from their shoulders down to their knees and were tied at the waist with some kind of cord. I understood this to be their traditional garb. The shards were no more. In front of each of us stood an intact and empty bowl.

How would you feel, if one second you were alone, and the next, you were sitting with four mysterious strangers who had inexplicably materialized out of nowhere? Scared? Freaked out? Of course. And I should have felt that way. But I didn't. I wasn't scared. I was calm. In fact, I couldn't remember a time that I felt so relaxed and at ease. Sitting there with the others, it was if there was nothing to worry about in the whole world; I was exactly where I was supposed to be.

The man on my left and the woman on my right reached out to me. Together, as a group, we clasped hands. The light from the Source grew stronger, brighter. The Source itself was moving faster now, shifting and twisting, intensifying, seemingly reacting to the bond we had formed. Warmth enveloped me. We unlatched our hands and the others reached down and gently held their bowls with a hand on each side. I did the same.

I did not see the material move from its source into my bowl, but when I looked down, it was there, swirling and spinning, restlessly hovering above the bottom of my bowl.

I turned to see if the others' bowls also contained the Source. There was no one there. I was alone, holding an empty bowl. The broken remnants of the other bowls were again cold shards lying lifelessly in fine dust, reflecting the glow of the Source gyrating within its rocky lair.

Before I had the chance to wrap my head around what had happened, I was shown something else. The Source began moving in a way I hadn't seen before. It rose up as one piece, until it hovered maybe eight inches above its basin. Then it began to spread out in all directions and become thinner, like dough being worked over by an invisible rolling pin. It was now about two feet wide and a foot and a half in height.

Two dark spots appeared, indefinable at first. Just two blurry blobs, each about three by five inches. One was more rectangular than the other and didn't move much. The other was bent in the middle, first forming a shape like an upside down "V", then straightening out like the other form.

The resolution sharpened and the blurry edges became clear. The spots became two figures, men, perfect in their miniature proportion. The two figures were in a tunnel, a tunnel that could have been anywhere, but looked and felt like it was in the catacomb under the Witch's Nose. The colors of the people, and of the rock within the cave, were not realistic; rather, they were all different hues of the color of the Source. There was bright gold, goldenrod, rusty yellow, a brownish metallic gold, many other shades that I couldn't name.

I knew the men. I knew where they came from, why they were there. The Source had preloaded this information into me and I hadn't even been conscious of it happening. I sat, watching and listening, as the Source showed me what once was.

Chapter XVII: Cyrus and Billy Bob

Their names were Cyrus and Billy Bob. They hailed from San Luis, Colorado, a small town that was originally a New Mexico territory. They met as gravediggers. Cyrus and Billy Bob struggled at odd jobs and were growing frustrated with their dead-end prospects when word got out that gold had been discovered at a place called Sutter's Mill, in California. It was Cyrus's idea to up and go. Most of the ideas came from Cyrus. There was no reason not to go. The year was 1848.

Billy Bob was short and stocky, with sinewy, powerful muscles toned from years of tough labor. He had never learned to read and write, which was not uncommon in those days, but still, he was embarrassed about it. Some men in the large group that had made their way over the Sierra Nevada mountains laughed at Billy Bob because he often paused before responding and spoke hesitantly. They nicknamed him "Slow Billy." Billy Bob was a proud man and this burned him inside, but Cyrus told him not to punch any of them in the face because it would jeopardize their place in the group.

If Billy Bob was the muscle, then Cyrus was the brains. He was tall and thin, almost gaunt, with weathered, brown skin darkened from years of working under the hot sun. He had piercing bright blue eyes that seemed to penetrate whomever he was speaking to. Cyrus had little physical strength but compensated with a sharp wit and quick tongue. Occasionally this would get him into trouble with other men, who mistook his big words for vanity or smugness.

Cyrus had taught himself to read and write, and always carried one book with him. It wasn't because he loved that book but because books were hard to come by and he hadn't the opportunity to find anything else. Sometimes at night in front of the campfire, Cyrus would read to Billy Bob.

Cyrus's book was called "The Little Mermaid," by Hans Christian Andersen. It was about five mermaids, sisters, who live in an underwa-

ter kingdom. Once a year, they get to visit the ocean's surface. During a violent storm, the youngest mermaid surfaces and witnesses a boat capsizing. She rescues a handsome prince from drowning and falls in love with him. As Cyrus read, Billy Bob would close his eyes, watching in his mind's eye the action and images, listening to the crackling and popping of the fire.

The journey through Utah and Nevada and into the Oregon Territory had been long and arduous. Three members of the party of twenty-four men had died along the way. When they finally arrived, Cyrus and Billy Bob discovered that the mining operation that had been set up was barely organized and not at all productive. The leader of the men had promised gold for everyone, early and often, yet very little had been discovered and mined, and fights often broke out among the men over who deserved which portion and why.

Cyrus and Billy Bob grew frustrated with their lack of involvement and decision-making within the group, but most of all, the lack of gold. They decided to splinter off from the group and try to make it on their own. It was a high risk, high reward move; traveling alone left them vulnerable to everything that was unknown about the Oregon Territory at that time - the weather, food supply, fresh water, how the native people would react if they came into contact with them. Still, Cyrus and Billy Bob were willing to take the risk. Early one morning, they sneaked off and disappeared into the woods.

The Source showed me Cyrus and Billy Bob standing near the same hole in the rock that I had climbed through. They each wore a backpack, from which hung tools that a miner of that time might have: shovel, pick, pan. Each pack had a rolled-up blanket strapped to the bottom of it.

Cyrus descended into the hole first, stepping slowly and carefully onto the first rung of the rope ladder, testing it with his weight, and then moving down to allow Billy Bob access. When they had both reached the bottom, Cyrus lit a gas lantern.

"Cyrus, w-what are we doin' down here?" Billy Bob asked, his high-pitched voice a mixture of anxiety and fear. He had a slight stutter when he was nervous or upset.

"You seen how old and sturdy that rope ladder was, Billy Bob?" Cyrus answered, his words echoing off the walls. "Know what that means? It means that this place is safe. It also means that people have been coming down here for a long time. There has to be a reason for that. I think that reason may be gold."

Cyrus's explanation seemed to calm Billy Bob. The two men adjusted their packs and headed off in the same direction I had gone, the light from the cave's entrance fading quickly behind them. They walked in silence, occasionally running their hands along the jagged edge of the cave wall, pausing when they had to decide which of two passageways to take and then heading out again, Cyrus in front, holding the lantern.

"What's it look like, Cyrus?"

"What's what look like?" They kept walking. Billy Bob didn't turn around.

"The gold." The word was said with equal parts excitement and frustration.

"Billy Bob, you've seen gold."

Cyrus knew this answer wouldn't satisfy him. They had traveled many miles over many months and all they had ever seen was a few tiny pieces in the bottom of a tin cup that one of the men with whom they had made their journey had panned from an almost-dry creek bed. They hadn't even been allowed to touch them.

"Yeah, I seen it," Billy Bob replied, hitching up his pants. "What I seen was a few pretty lousy crumbs. I didn't come out all this way for

104

that. I want to know what gold looks like, feels like in my hand. I want to touch it."

"I held a nugget in my hand once." The quiet crunch of boots on the tunnel floor swallowed the fading echo of Cyrus's words.

"You did?" asked Billy Bob. "Where? You never tol' me!"

"Before we left Colorado, months back," Cyrus explained, trying to make it sound matter of fact. "One of the guys had it, said he won it in a poker game."

Cyrus waited for Billy Bob to ask more questions. But he didn't. They walked on, the light from their lantern casting distorted shadows along the cavern walls.

"It was smooth, very smooth," started Cyrus again.

"What was?" asked Billy Bob.

"The gold!" snapped Cyrus. He rarely got frustrated with Billy Bob, but the long trip and lack of positive results had begun to wear on him. They stopped, took off their packs, and sat, placing the lantern equidistant in front of them.

"S-sorry, Cyrus."

"No, I'm sorry for snapping at ya', Billy Bob. It's just -"

"I know," nodded Billy Bob.

"Anyway, about the gold," Cyrus continued. "It was smooth, almost velvety." The lantern's yellow light flickered in Cyrus's tired blue eyes. Billy Bob settled in to listen. To him, it felt like they were sitting at the campfire, Cyrus reading to him from the book. Instinctively, Billy Bob closed his eyes to listen and to see.

"We were outside, packing for the trip, when one of the guys - Caleb, you know him - asked me to follow him over to a grove of Bristlecone pines. I did. He took what I thought was a small rock out of his pocket.

"He held it out, palm up. It was maybe four inches from top to bottom, oblong - "

"Oblong?" Billy Bob interrupted. "What's that?"

It's kinda peanut shaped, I guess. But a big peanut. About… half an inch thick, with a notch on one side. He handed it to me."

"Tell me about it," Billy Bob asked, closing his eyes again like he was entering a dream. "Tell me everything about it."

"Like I was sayin', it was smooth," Cyrus began, elongating the vowels in the word. "So smooth that, when I turned it over in my hand, it didn't really feel like I was touchin' it at all."

"Whaddya mean?" inquired Billy Bob, furrowing his brow, his eyes still shut.

"Hard to describe, but it felt like it had a, well, had a skin, so that I wasn't really touchin' the gold at all, but only the outer surface of it. Like a barrier."

"Barrier?" Billy Bob opened one eye.

"Somethin' that won't let you in."

They unstrapped their canteens from their packs and took a couple of swigs. Cyrus pulled out a piece of deer jerky ("It never spoils," he had told Billy Bob as they packed for their trip, weeks before), used the medium blade of his pocket knife to cut it in half, and handed some to his traveling companion. Billy Bob ripped a small piece off with his teeth.

"How heavy was it, Cyrus?" asked Billy Bob between bites.

"Didn't have a scale," Cyrus said, chewing.

"I mean, was it heavy? Heavy in your hand?"

"Lighter than I thought it would be," responded Cyrus, strapping his canteen on to his pack. He stood and looked down at Billy Bob.

"I wish you had shown it to me," said Billy Bob, dejected. Cyrus ignored the comment.

"Our kerosene won't last forever." It was the signal to get going. Billy Bob stood, put his pack on over one shoulder, and stretched his arms out wide, yawning.

"You see somethin', Cyrus?" He had yet to stand.

"Nope."

"Down there." Billy Bob pointed.

"Your eyes are most likely playin' tricks, Billy Bob," said Cyrus. "Maybe it's the lantern's light bouncin' around in here. We've been in the dark for a while now."

"It ain't the lantern, Cyrus." Billy Bob was adamant. "It's a glow, a yellow glow. Ya' think it's gold?" His words buzzed with excitement.

"No, gold doesn't glow."

Cyrus crouched down and adjusted the governor on the lantern, reducing the intensity of the flame. He straightened up again, squinting against the darkness in the direction that Billy Bob had gestured.

"I think I see something too," he said. "Let's go take a look."

Cyrus and Billy Bob made their way down the tunnel. The glow grew stronger as they approached the split. Billy Bob hung back a few feet, seemingly anxious about what they might find. If gold didn't glow, and this was glowing, then what was it?

The vista in front of me blurred. The Source began to move, slowly at first, like a bowl of cookie dough being mixed with a big spoon, around, in, out, then faster, Cyrus and Billy Bob becoming part of the vibrating swirl, twisting and inverting on itself, until no details remained and the Source had returned to the non-shape in which I had found it, floating silently above its resting place in the wall of the tunnel.

I felt like I had been sitting for hours. Maybe I had. I stood, legs stiff, unsure of what to do. All I had seen and the people I had sat with and Cyrus and Billy Bob bounced around in my brain. Somehow, the Source knew the past, and could show the past. But - what was it? Where did it come from?

As I struggled to understand how I had seen what I had seen, the Source began to re-form. It was taking a shape again, one I recognized from the first moments that I had been shown Billy Bob and Cyrus: it was the Witch's Nose. But it was more than that. It was a view of the mountain itself, or more accurately, a view into or through the mountain. I could see an entire network of the tunnels, how each connected to the others, like an x-ray. The source had shown me a complete three-dimensional model. I saw where I had entered, in which tunnels I had traveled. Then the Source revealed to me the two places that saved my life. It displayed my location in the tunnels, and the way out.

With the route out of the tunnels seared in my brain, I left the Source and felt my way along the tunnel walls. Left, left, right. Where the tunnel splits, right again. The images of the people whose hands I had held were fresh in my mind, the voices of Cyrus and Billy Bob still crystal clear. And in the distance, a light, but this one different, growing bigger, brighter. I was out. I had made it.

Chapter XVIII: Back to Reality

I turned the last page over. Nothing. That was all there was, or at least all Frank wanted to show me. I looked up. He was a few feet from me, facing away and hunched over, folding up the metal rack on which the steak had been cooked. I got the impression that, although he had probably read the letters many times, he had been listening intently. It's always different when someone is reading to you.

I sat, my legs still dangling down into the hole, feeling like a visitor, an outsider. I couldn't think of anything to say. Frank was putting the rack back into his pack and adjusting something. Then he walked over to me and reached out his hand. For a second, I thought he was offering to help me up. But he had given me a flashlight a couple hours before and was just asking for it back.

"Can I ask you a question?"

"What." He stood, his back to me, on the edge of the rock, overlooking the valley. He was listening.

"What happened after your father left the passageways?"

There was no answer. I tried something else. "In order to pass his yitcarese, your father - "

"Warrant Officer," Frank interrupted. "You will refer to him as Warrant Officer. And you don't *pass* yitcarese; you complete it. You become a man."

"Sorry," I said. "For Warrant Officer to complete his yitcarese, he needed to spend three days alone. The letter to you has him being chased up to the Witch's Nose that first day, en-

110

tering the tunnels, and...well, it didn't at all sound like he spent more than maybe one night down there."

"Warrant Officer was gone for three days," he said defensively, turning around toward me. His response contained no evidence, nor explanation. It made no sense. But I believed him.

"On the afternoon of the third day, some villagers found Warrant Officer wandering in the woods, hungry, dirty. They brought him back to my grandfather. The elders determined that he had successfully completed his yitcarese. Warrant Officer was a man who gave his life for his country."

"And his ip-sah-keen?" I asked. ""Was it the fox?"

"That was not shared with me."

It was always difficult to figure out how Frank was feeling, unless he was angry. It was also hard to know if he was lying. About the ip-sah-keen, I think he was. He must have known. But why lie?

"So," Frank started, "would you agree that I have answered the questions you had for me?"

"Yes, I would," I responded, warily. Where was he going with this?

"Now I have a question for you."

The moon had come out from behind the clouds, painting the rock ledges and chaparral on the Witch's Nose a cold, alien gray. The fog that surrounded us made it seem like we were on our own little planet, floating silently above the valley floor, isolated. I had never spent time with someone who made me feel so alone.

Frank sat down across from me again, legs bent at the knee, feet disappearing into the almost-perfect rock hole. He leaned forward, holding the flashlight so that the beam of light hit each step of the rope ladder on its way down to the floor of the tunnel, far below.

"Do you know why I took you here?" Frank didn't take his eyes off of the light and the ladder.

"No," I told him.

"Did you think you were the first person besides me to read the letter?" he asked. "To know what happened down there?"

"Yes."

"You're right," he replied. For a moment, I allowed myself to feel special, or proud, or something like that.

"Why do you think I allowed you to come up here, to walk this sacred ground, and learn about the history of my family, and of the Source?"

It hit me then. There could only be one reason. Then, as if on cue with my realization, the beam of light hit me in the face. It was as if Frank knew the precise moment that I had figured it out. I shielded my face with my hand and looked across at him. He clicked off the flashlight. Dark again.

"That's right, kal-san-gip," he said, condescendingly. "You know now."

Frank had used that word in the woods when we had first met, and I knew it had a negative meaning. I didn't want to hear what I knew he was going to tell me.

"What does "kal-san-gip" mean?"

"There's no direct translation into English," he said, clicking the flashlight off and on like a metronome. "But I suppose the closest you could get would be, 'boy that knows nothing.' 'Kal-san-gip' describes someone just starting out, just beginning their journey, who doesn't yet know what they will face."

He was right. I was a 'kal-san-gip.' Before I had read the Warrant Officer's letters, I had known nothing. And I still knew very little. As for my journey, I wasn't even sure what my journey was. Or if I even had one.

"And because you are a 'kal-san-gip,'" Frank continued, "you will be helpful. You come with no predetermined opinions, no judgments. You're a blank page.

The Source is the only connection I have with Warrant Officer," he said. "He had to go down there alone. He had no choice. There was no other option. But I have an option. It's you." Déjà vu.

"Why?" I asked him. "Why do you want to do it?"

"Wow, you really are a 'kal-san-gip.'"

"Ok, I'm a 'kal-san-gip.' Fine. You'll get no argument from me," I said, feeling irritated for putting myself in this position. "But I'd like an answer."

"Don't get mouthy," Frank warned.

"Sorry." Not sorry.

"I will never complete my yitcarese," he said. "But I can go where my father was, sit where my father sat, see what he saw."

For a moment, I looked at Frank and saw a human being. I could understand the emotion behind the words. But I blurted out a non sequitur.

"Does Mama know about this place?"

Frank made sure I knew he thought it was a stupid question by waiting an extra second before responding. "This has nothing to do with Mama," he said dismissively, standing up again, a silhouette in blurry darkness against the once-again moon. I stood too. I thought about my mom, and about the intruder. A shiver caught me.

"Mama will be expecting us," I said, sounding like a whiny sibling ready to tell on his big brother.

"We're not going in tonight, zah-tah-juh," he said, walking away from me until I couldn't see him anymore. Only his voice remained.

"I promised Mama we'd go to your place, and I will keep that promise. We'll camp here on the rock tonight, and head out at first light. Then, we'll return to Mama's, check and restock supplies, and return here."

"What if I refuse?" I asked him.

"You can't refuse," he said. "You won't refuse. You owe me. Search your heart. You know it's true. Besides, you'd never make it out here on your own. We both know that." He was right. We both did. Awkward pause. Change the subject.

"What does 'zah-tah-juh' mean?"

"Oh, that," he replied, matter-of-factly. "That word has been used by The Original People for many generations."

"So, what is it?"

"Zah-tah-juh?" Frank had heard me clearly. He was just messing with me now.

"Yeah. What's it mean?"

"Dumb ass."

A snort emanated from the darkness. Then another. Then a honk, followed by two quick snorts. For the first time, I heard Frank Summers laugh.

Chapter XIX: The Other Frank

I don't remember marching down the Witch's Nose as first light broke over the woods. I couldn't recall hitting the switchbacks. I walked past the Fork, a place of so much power, and barely noticed it.

I became aware of what was going on when the straps of my pack began digging into my upper back and I began to sweat. I was hungry. It was then that I realized that we were already well on our way back up to my place.

My place. Where three days ago - it felt like three years - my mom drove away and left me alone for the first time. What would have happened had I not tried to pick up that extra piece of wood? One thing was for certain: I wouldn't be here, marching in the morning heat behind this person.

But I also would not have met Desiree. When I thought of her name, of her short hair, her weird, dark make-up, her dimples, I felt...I don't know. Maybe I just *felt*. When Desiree floated through my mind, I forgot about the human metronome marching in front of me, forgot about my aching body, about the stranger I had run from a few days before.

Suddenly, there she was: my mom. She was dumping a dustpan of broken glass into a trash can, looking up, calling my name, running to me, hugging me. After what seemed like minutes, she pulled away from me, her hands still latched onto my shoulders. She looked at me, then at Frank. Then back at me.

"What's going on?" she asked. "Who is this?" Her voice was flat, almost practiced. The words were right; the emotion wasn't. It was like she had almost been anticipating this conversation.

"Right after you left," I began to explain, "I slipped and fell on the steps down by the woodpile. A couple pieces of wood landed on me and I was knocked out. Next thing I know, I was inside the house. It was dark out. A fire was burning in the hearth. There was a man."

"A man?" she asked. "Who?"

"I don't know," I said, looking over at Frank, who hadn't spoken. "He was big. I felt like I was in danger."

I expected her to keep pressing me for details - about the broken bedroom window, the cut power cable. She didn't. Instead, she turned to Frank, who had just finished tucking his shirt in and was holding his hat between his knees and smoothing back his hair. The gun and holster were gone from his hip; I assumed he had moved them into his pack.

"Who is this?" my mom asked me, looking at Frank.

I gestured toward Frank. "This is - "

"Frank Summers is the name, ma'am," he said, interrupting me. He approached my mother and extending his hand. "Pleasure to meet you." His words were light and clear and dripping with politeness. They shook hands.

"Danny has told me a lot about you." He maintained eye contact throughout.

"Most of it good, I hope."

"All of it," he lied, smiling. She smiled back. My mother was actually flattered by this polite stranger. They continued to chat, their words lost in the gentle breeze that rustled the trees overhead. Who *was* this person, and what had he done with

117

Frank? In front of me, smiling, nodding, stood the exact opposite of the passive-aggressive sociopath I knew: a charming,
well-spoken teenage boy, skilled in social graces, making small
talk. I did not know this Frank, this walking, talking oxymo-
ron. I tuned back in just in time to hear:

"…would have been in big trouble had I not found him. He
was hungry, thirsty, and tired, and that part of the woods is no-
torious for bears."

Wow. Frank hadn't believed me when I told Mama of my
encounter with the bear the night I had slept in the crook of the
tree, overlooking the creek. Now, here he was, playing it like he
was my protector. If I wanted my mom to know the truth, about
how Frank had *captured* me, the forced march to Mama's, the
bear, I would have to talk to her alone. But even if I did, who
would she believe: me, the boy who couldn't even handle his
first night alone, or the older, kind, charismatic, young man prat-
tling on in front of her?

And what else would I tell her? About the letters? The
Witch's Nose? Warrant Officer's yitcarese? The Source? It all
sounded like so much fantasy, the science fiction dreams of a
twelve-year-old boy.

But Desiree was real, that much I knew. And if I was going
to see her again, I would have to leave with Frank in the morning and return to Mama's. So my dilemma was this: If I told my
mom the truth about Frank, about what had happened while I
was gone, and she believed me, then there was no way she
would let me leave with Frank. Desiree might have left Mama's
place before I ever got the chance to get back there. I wouldn't
know where she had gone, and I doubted Mama would be able
to tell me, even if she knew.

118

On the other hand, if I said nothing, Frank would say something. He wouldn't climb down the rope ladder into the black tunnels beneath the Witch's Nose alone. He needed me. So Frank would look my mother straight in the eye and invent a reason that he needed me to return to Mama's place with him, if only for a few days. It would make perfect and logical sense but would have no basis in reality whatsoever. And my mom would believe him.

And I wouldn't be upset. Because I needed Frank. I needed him to get me back to Mama's place, to see Desiree. I knew now that I had to see her. Didn't just want to. Needed to. It was scary, this feeling. Scary mixed with something else, something good, I couldn't put words to, like the clickety-clack of a wooden roller coaster slowly climbing, the car pausing at the top, not knowing what would happen or when or what it would feel like when you finally felt yourself falling. I was beginning to fall.

I never did talk to my mom. Not in any real detail, anyway. I told her a little about Mama's place, but that's all. We didn't talk about Frank, or about what happened after I ran from the property. And certainly not about what I had learned about Frank's family and what may still lie inside the big rock, miles across the canyon from us. And definitely not about Desiree.

After dinner, Frank disappeared into the woods. Exactly where, I don't know. I thought of looking for him but then wasn't sure I wanted to know what he was doing out there.

When it got late, Frank took my room (my mom insisted on it) and I took the couch. I couldn't sleep. Instead, I sat in front of the fire, watching the flames die and trying not to think. It didn't work.

Chapter XX: Getting Ready

I finally did fall asleep, and I don't think I moved all night. One of those coma sleeps. I woke up to the sound of Frank' boots pounding across the floor. I heard the door open and close and sat up.

I looked through the living room window. Frank wasn't far from my mom's pickup. He had emptied the contents of the two backpacks and was methodically repacking them. I watched him for a while. The thought of the hike back down to Mama's weighed on me. On the other hand, I would get to see Desiree.

My mom poured us bowls of cereal and made toast, then left for her bedroom. I wasn't hungry. Frank came back in. I gestured to him that there was food on the table. We sat down. He went right to his napkin and began to fold. Maybe he had to fold it. Maybe it wasn't even a choice for him.

"You ready for another walk in the woods, 'zah-tah-juh'?" Frank said, taking a neatly controlled bite of his cereal.

"As much as I ever will be," I said. His attitude didn't even bother me. Maybe I was getting used to it. I briefly considered picking up Frank's bowl of cereal and milk and dumping it on his head, then thought better of it.

He finished his cereal, stood, took his hat off and smoothed his hair. Then he tucked in his shirt for the four hundredth time since I had met him and patted down imaginary wrinkles in his camouflage pants. My mom appeared.

"Do you two want me to pack you lunch?" she asked. I shrugged. Frank crowed, "No thank you ma'am, we'll be fine."

As we walked outside, Frank in front, I was overcome with a sudden urge to tell my mom everything. I managed to whisper a desperate but meager, "We need to talk!" If she heard me, she didn't react.

Frank never told me what he said to my mom that convinced her to let me leave with him. Whatever it was, it worked. We were on our way back to Mama's place- and I was headed back to Desiree.

Chapter XXI: Back to Mama's

The first couple of hours of the return hike were eerily quiet. I kept pace ten yards behind Frank. We hardly spoke, which wasn't surprising. Even the nature surrounding us seemed subdued. No breeze through the trees. The mountains looked like green paint on canvas. There wasn't a cloud in the sky, but the stillness in the air felt like the calm before the storm.

Frank's deep voice jarred me from my thoughts. "Recognize this place?" he asked. I did. I had settled into a rhythm and pace that allowed me to keep up with Frank's robotic march but hadn't really been paying attention to where we were. We had come upon the creek where I had climbed the tree that first night away from home. It's branches still hung over the water, which had receded a bit.

While Frank pulled off his pack, I walked over to the tree. I wanted to look at the scratch marks the bear had left, for no other reason than to be sure that it had actually happened.

Frank was taking a leak, his back to me, twenty yards away. I was on the opposite side of the tree that the bear had scratched. What if I walked around to the other side of the tree and there were no scratches? What would that mean? That there hadn't been a bear?

But it did happen. I remembered it. And I could even call Frank over to show him the scratches, because he consistently doubted my story of being chased by the intruder, and the scratches would add credibility to what I knew had happened to me. The marks were there, deep vertical slashes in the soft brown and green bark. I ran my fingers along the fresh splintered edges and turned to look back at Frank. He was already gearing back up, having rested no more than a couple minutes. I wouldn't tell him about the scratches. It wouldn't change anything.

It was well past dark when we finally made it back to Mama's. I had no idea what time it was. In fact, I hadn't been keeping track of time since the night I had thrown the chair through the window of my mother's room and run from the house.

Frank and I went straight to the shed and unloaded our packs. Acer was there. Frank watched as he jumped up and turned in circles, excited to see me, pushing his body sideways against my knee, asking for attention. I did my best to ignore Acer, silently promising him that I would give him some love and a treat later.

I left Frank and headed up the stairs to the sliding door. The house was dark. I moved toward the kitchen to find a bite to eat. I could almost hear Frank's "...and it's MY kitchen!" To my left, down the darkened hall, a tiny slit of light glowed from underneath Desiree's door. She was up.

I didn't turn on the light in the kitchen. In the fridge I found some leftover spaghetti with red sauce, which I wolfed down without even bothering to warm it up. I followed that up with a too-tart apple, although I didn't remember seeing an apple tree on the property. I finished off the quick meal with a glass of water. Mountain water had a mineral taste to it that I could never quite get used to.

I walked back to the glass door to see if Frank was still down at the shed. The door to it was closed but the light was still on, casting its square-shaped pale yellow onto Desiree's flats. The backpacks and other supplies were no longer on the ground outside; there was no evidence to suggest we had ever gone anywhere.

I walked down the hall to Desiree's door, the smell of burn-ing candles coming from within. I wondered if I should knock or whisper. I felt like she knew I was there, so I didn't do either.

"Come."

I pushed on the door. Desiree was sitting on the bed, hold-ing the writing pad, surrounded by crumpled up pieces of bind-er paper, some on her, some on the bed, some on the floor, like giant popcorn. The chair was still lying on its side, the bed co-vers now almost completely kicked under the bed. There were four candles in clear glass votive jars burning on the little table, each perched precariously on top of a hand-shaped mound of dirt from the spilled plant.

"So?" she asked, like I was late with a report or some-thing. She didn't look up.

"So, what?" I asked. Now she looked up.

"So, how did it go?"

It was a short question that would require a long answer if I was going to share everything that had happened on the hike, but I knew that, at the very least, I had to tell her about the letter Frank had me read, from Warrant Officer Franklin Summers.

Desiree bounded off of the bed and jumped to her feet, paper popcorn flying. She picked up two candles from their little dirt perches and sat down again, on the side closest to the knocked-over plant. She put one down and held the other one maybe six inches in front of her face.

"Pull up that chair," she told me, her almond eyes never leaving the flickering flame. I righted the chair and sat across from her.

"It's pretty, huh?" she asked.

"Yeah, pretty." I looked at Desiree through the flame. I wanted to say *you're pretty*. But I didn't.

"Do you know what the hottest part of a flame is?" She knew I didn't. "Come closer." I scooted in. Our faces were a foot away from each other. At that moment, if time had somehow stopped and I was forced to stay like that forever, I would have been happy.

"Take a guess," she said.

"The red part," I responded, the breath of my answer bending the flame toward her. "Red means hot."

"Red does mean hot," Desiree said. "But not in a flame." She read more than I. She knew more than I did. She was smarter than I was. But she was never condescending about it. I had two more guesses.

"Yellow?"

"Actually, the hottest part of the flame is the blue part. It's the section that is completely combusting, burning up all the oxygen."

"That's cool." I was feeling slightly less stupid about my responses when she asked me things.

"The blue part is called the non-luminous zone," she continued. "Non-luminous, as in not the part that's the brightest."

"But it's the hottest," I said. I was trying to understand what she was getting at. Trying.

"Blow it out."

I inhaled. She was looking at me. The instant before I blew, Desiree squeezed the wick between her index finger and thumb and the flame disappeared into a puff of gray smoke. And then the laugh. It defied gravity.

"Ok," she said, putting down the candle and dusting off invisible ashes from her jeans, "I want to know what happened, from the time you and Frank left."

"Well, first of all," I said, "Frank knows."

"He knows what?"

"He knows we read Warrant Officer's letters."

"How?" she asked. "Did you tell him?"

"Of course not," I replied, wondering why she would have even thought that was a possibility. "He followed us into the woods."

"Was he pissed?" she asked me. Learning about Frank spying on us didn't seem to have flustered her.

"He's hated me from the second he saw me," I said. "I don't think anything could make him angrier than he has always been, not even invading his privacy and learning his secrets."

I left out most of the boring hiking parts. I told her about the map, about our discussion about the Original People. I left out the part about almost collapsing from exhaustion and Frank dumping water on me.

But most of the time, I focused on the letter. I described how Frank had led me to the Witch's Nose, that he had handed me the last letter from his father and told me to read it, and that I felt helpless not to.

"The letter started with Franklin, Frank's father, describing the lead up to his *yitcarese*. He was nervous, wasn't sure he could do it. And there was no one he could talk to about it."

"Why not?" Desiree asked.

"Against tribal tradition," I said. "You were pretty much on your own. Plus, the *yitcarese* is really an experience of personal discovery. When a young man returns from it, he is forbidden to talk about it. So, it was weird that this letter even existed."

"Warrant Officer writes about his *yitcarese* in the letter?"

"Well first, Warrant Officer tells Frank that he understands if Frank doesn't want to continue reading, that it goes against tribal rules. But then he describes the entire thing."

"Wow."

"Yeah. That was pretty much my reaction, too."

"So go ahead," she said. "Tell me."

"Things got off to a good start for Warrant Officer," I continued. "The weather was good. Plenty of water, and he had success identifying and foraging for food. But all of a sudden, he's being chased by a bear. He runs for his life and also keeps seeing this little gray fox in front of him. He thinks it might be his *ip-sah-keen* but isn't sure."

"You're good at summarizing," Desiree said, shifting to sitting cross-legged on her bed. It was my first compliment from her, and it felt good. My cheeks and forehead felt warm. I hoped she couldn't tell. I kept talking.

"Warrant Officer climbs this hill, powered by fear of the bear. He thinks the area is familiar but not until reaching the top does he realize he's at the Witch's Nose.

"The fox is there, like it's been waiting for him. He sees this hole in the rock. It's got a rope ladder. He decides that, despite the danger, going down into the hole is his only real way of making sure the bear doesn't get him."

"Wait, hold on," Desiree said, propping herself up against the wall with a pillow. "Where were you when you were reading Warrant Officer's letter to Frank?"

"We were there, at the Witch's Nose," I said.

"What?" She bolted upright and leaned toward me.

"Yeah, we were there," I said. "With our legs dangling down into the hole." Desiree had a far off look in her eye. She wasn't listening. She was somewhere else. I waited.

Then she was back. She took a purple bandana from the desk drawer, folded it over a few times, and wrapped it around her head, tying it off in back. Two words were written on the bandana in black: 'pretty' on one side and 'smart' on the other. I couldn't think of two better words to describe her.

"Ok, fire away," she told me. "Then what?"

"He climbs down the rope ladder and reaches the bottom. He's got nothing: no food, no water, no light. He starts walking, and it gets dark in a hurry - really dark. He's lost in a series of tunnels that connect to each other inside of the mountain.

"He wanders for a while, becoming more and more lost. It's darker than anything he's ever experienced. There's no light, so there's nothing for his eyes to adjust to. He's losing hope about finding his *ip-sah-keen*, about completing his *yitcarese*, even about ever getting out.

"But something inside of him doesn't let him give up. He continues feeling his way through the caverns. And the story gets...gets..."

"Gets what?" Desiree asked excitedly.

"Gets - weird." I struggled to find the words. "Almost unbelievable."

"Do *you* believe it?" she asked me.

Did I? The idea that Warrant Officer had made up what he had described happened to him inside the Witch's Nose, with all the amazing detail, didn't feel right. There was no reason to create such a detailed lie. But most importantly, when I searched my soul, the story felt true.

"Yes," I responded to her. "I believe it."

"An unbelievable, but true, story," Desiree said, rubbing her hands together. "Those are my favorite. Continue, Danny." I loved it when she called me that. I took a deep breath.

"Ok. So, Warrant Officer sits for a long time. He's not sure for how long. He has a choice to make: either just give up and die down there or get up and keep going.

"Something inside of him makes him continue. He feels his way along the walls in pitch black. Then he sees something." I paused, thinking about what, or how, I was going to describe what happened next.

Desiree interrupted my thoughts. "Danny, what do you mean, 'he sees something'?" You said it was totally dark down there."

"It was," I said. "Pitch black."

"So how could he see something?"

"It was light," I answered, realizing how stupid that sounded.

"It was light?" Desiree asked. "What was light?"

"The thing he saw." My recall of Warrant Officer's *yitcarese* was a poor replacement for the real thing, but I struggled on.

"It's a glow, a yellowish glow. He thinks he's hallucinating. He figures it might be someone else down there who had a lantern or lit a fire, but as he approaches it, he realizes that it's not." I don't know how I got through describing what Warrant Officer saw next. I just kept talking, trying to not think about what Desiree was thinking. I tried to explain to Desiree what the Source looked like, what it did. I recounted the sense of peace that came over Warrant Officer when he grasped hands with the ancient people who materialized after he righted the pottery bowl.

I spent the most time revealing in as much detail as I could the story of Cyrus and Billy Bob, the two struggling gold miners. Recalling for Desiree their background and words and actions was the easy part; explaining how the images and sound

130

came from a golden liquid-like substance levitating above a bowl-shaped rock was more difficult.

I talked for at least an hour. Desiree sat cross-legged on the bed, her back straight and body still, looking at me and listening. Her expression was serious and focused, but impossible to read. I wondered if any of what I was saying made sense.

Finally, I finished. She didn't move. Neither did I. The quiet was a physical presence between us. Then suddenly she jumped to her feet, everything changing, the opposite of what it was just a moment before.

"You know what this means, right, Danny?" Her voice had an intensity and focus I had never heard from her.

"What does it mean?"

"We need to go." Her voice had a manic quality.

"Go?"

"Yeah, go inside!" she continued. "Into the tubes."

"The tubes?"

"What are you, a broken record? Yes, the *tubes*. The tunnels. To find it. To take it. Or at least some of it."

There was a finality to her words, like it had already been decided and now only the details were left to discuss.

"Maybe we should just - leave it." The words bubbled up from me. She looked at me like I was an alien that had just beamed down from a spaceship and materialized in front of her.

"Just leave it?" she asked, incredulous, her mouth agape. "Just *leave* it?"

"Yeah, leave it there," I said. "It's been there for, I don't know, thousands of years maybe. Maybe it's not meant to come out, not meant to be - anywhere besides where it is."

"Look," Desiree said, ignoring my suggestion, "this *means* something to me. I don't know what, but it's like I've been *waiting* for this. I know it sounds strange, but I *have* to go. And I can't do it on my own. You're here. You're it. You're all I've got. You're *going*."

Suddenly it was like I didn't have a say. But I *did* have a say. I could say no. She couldn't *make* me go. But my fear of the tunnels was losing out to the desire to spend time with her. Hearing that she needed me felt good. No one had ever needed me before. Not like her. Not like this. But there was a problem. Frank. Always Frank.

"Frank's taking me down there," I said to her.

"Did he tell you that?" she asked.

"Yes. He said I owed it to him. For digging up the letters and reading them, for violating his privacy."

"That wasn't your fault, Danny," she replied. "It was mine." Was she offering to take my place? I waited for her words to make sense. They didn't.

"So, *you'll* go with him, not me?" I asked. She squinted her eyes at me and tilted her head like it was the most ridiculous thing she had ever heard.

"Hell, no," she said. "Screw that."

She was simply cutting Frank out of the equation. Period. End of story. I let that sink in. Desiree's eyes were closed. I wondered what she was thinking. Was she thinking about our route to the Witch's Nose? About our supplies?

I was thinking about how important it was to Frank to follow in his father's steps. How it seemed like that was all he cared about, and how he was counting on me to go with him. "How will we sneak out of here without him knowing?" I asked. "We failed last time."

"No, we didn't." The words came out quick and smooth, confidently. She still hadn't opened her eyes.

"We didn't?" I asked her, disagreeing. "He followed us. He saw us. He was watching the whole time."

"And?" A sly smile. Mind games. So we didn't fail, which meant...

"You *knew*?" I was incredulous. "You knew he followed us?"

"I suspected. Wasn't sure."

"Why?" I asked. "Why did we go if you thought he would follow us?"

"I don't have an answer, Danny," she said. "Switch."

"Switch?"

"Yeah, you take the bed, I'll take the chair."

We switched. I didn't ask why. I was beginning to learn that the *why* of things wasn't all that important to Desiree.

"When he finds out - "

"*If* he finds out," she interrupted.

"Ok, *if* he finds out, he'll be pissed."

"Weren't you the one who told me that he couldn't be any angrier with you?" The smile again. Innocent. Devious. It blurred the point I wanted to make, made me forget my arguments. Amnesia masquerading as almond-shaped eyes.

"I don't know how to get there." I was running out of reasons to refuse.

"Don't worry, I've got a pretty good idea where it is," she said.

"How will we know we'll be safe?" Couldn't think of a wimpier thing to ask.

"We'll know." Her answer made no sense. I accepted it.

"Isn't it scary?" Again, coming across as a real tough guy.

"That's all between your ears," she said, tapping her index fingers against her temples.

"What if the Source isn't there anymore?" I asked Desiree. "The letter from Frank's father described events that happened a long time ago."

"First off, why wouldn't it be there?" she responded. "If it was there during the Gold Rush, and Cyrus and..."

"Billy Bob."

"...and Billy Bob had seen it, then why would it be gone *now*?" She looked at me like she expected me to provide her a complete explanation. I couldn't.

"Besides," she continued, standing up and looking down at me, "what's the worst thing that could happen? When we get down into the tubes, the Source is gone. Big deal. You know what we call this kind of situation, Danny?"

"What?"

"A win-win." I rolled that over in my brain. Desiree had twisted the whole thing into a "win-win." She opened the desk drawer and pulled out a black Sharpie and looked for a blank space on the wall. She located one, by the foot of the bed, and started writing some words. She was already on to the next thing.

"When will we go?" I was running out of questions.

"Tomorrow. After breakfast. I'll sneak down to the shed to-night and pack us up." It was settled. We would go. And I had put up little resistance.

"What's with the lines and stars?" she asked me, turning away from her spot on the wall and pointing to the desk. "Why do you always make that?"

I looked down. I had taken the two remaining candles off the dirt piles and spread out the dirt. Into it I had carved two parallel, straight lines, about six inches apart. In between the lines I had made ten marks. Each mark had five points to it, like little stars.

"I don't know," I said. "I'm never conscious of it."

Chapter XXII: Just Walking the Dog

It was dark out, but I sensed morning already. I'm not sure I slept. Thoughts wouldn't stop circulating in my brain; about Frank mostly, and what he would do if he caught us at the Witch's Nose. I had a feeling that our trip to the tubes might be the last straw for Frank, that his rage would finally boil over. Then we would experience his full wrath, whatever form that might take. But Desiree didn't seem worried about him. Then again, she never seemed worried about much.

The other reason I could barely sleep had nothing to do with Frank. It had to do with Acer. He insisted on sleeping next to me. I was surprised that Frank even let him sleep indoors, given his Neanderthal attitudes toward pets. Acer would hop onto the couch, sniff a few times, spin two or three slow 360s, lie down, turn on his side, and fall asleep. I'd push him off. He'd jump up. We repeated this dance I don't know how many times. Finally, I gave up. Acer snored and didn't smell great, but he was warm.

Desiree had told me that we were to leave at daybreak, so I wanted to be ready. On the way to the kitchen, I walked past Frank's room. The door was open a crack. I peeked in. He was sleeping on his back, his covers tucked in tightly around him. If you've ever seen a photograph of the sarcophagus of King Tut, the way he's lying there on his back, sightless eyes staring skyward, perfectly still, then you know what Frank looked like that morning.

"Morning, Danny."

Mama was up bright and early, sitting at the dining room table with a bunch of papers spread out in front of her. She had on a bathrobe and slippers. Steam rose from a mug of coffee.

136

"Good morning," I replied sleepily.

"How's that couch?" she asked.

"It's ok," I lied. Desiree walked in, shooting me a quick glance that showed no evidence of our secret.

"What do you two have planned today?" Mama inquired, taking a sip of her coffee.

I answered her in my mind with the ridiculous truth: *We're going to enter an ancient tunnel system to search for a material that defies the known laws of physics and can show us the past.*

"We're gonna take Acer out for a while, hike the property," Desiree said, walking into the kitchen. I stood awkwardly at the table, off to the side from Mama, watching her sort the papers into piles.

"Danny," Desiree called from the kitchen, "come grab some grub before we go."

"Desiree," said Mama, "you know how Frank feels about that dog. Did you ask him?" I heard the fridge close. Desiree walked back in.

"I'm not taking Acer, at least officially," she explained, while twisting the bag of a loaf of bread in her hand. "Danny and I are going to take off. We won't call him. So, if he follows us, that's not on us. We're just walkin.' So, I don't need to ask Frank." This girl was good.

"Suit yourself," replied Mama, returning to her papers.

Desiree motioned to me to join her as she walked back to the kitchen. I heard the doggy door in the mudroom open. In burst

Acer, hyperactive and heavy-breathing. His wagging tail smacked my legs as he pushed up against me.

"That dog likes you," Desiree said, popping down two slices of bread into the toaster.

"Sometimes I wish he didn't," I said. She raised her eyebrows like she was saying, *Oh well, there are worse problems to have.* She went to the fridge and pulled out a cube of butter and a carton of eggs, handing me both. "Whip us up some scrambled," she said.

I didn't know where anything was kept, so I just opened up cupboards and drawers until I found the supplies I needed. I cracked open and scrambled the eggs. Desiree made sandwiches, four of them, and put them into paper bags, along with a couple of bananas and apples and some chips. I recognized the canteens. They were the ones Frank and I used on our hike to the Witch's Nose. Desiree filled them with ice cubes and topped them off with water from the sink.

We sat at the table and ate breakfast. Mama had cleared off her stuff and left the room. But we were only alone for a second. The sliding glass door opened and Frank walked in.

"Where are you two going?" he asked, making no effort to mask his disgust with the prospect.

"Nunya," Desiree replied, pushing her eggs around the plate with the fork.

"*Nunya?*" Frank asked, instantly angry and perplexed. "Where the hell is that?"

"Nunya business," she said.

138

Oh boy. I took a bite of eggs and didn't look up. Desiree had returned his sour attitude with an equally rude and sarcastic comment. Would he yell at her? Or would there be something worse?

Frank looked down at both of us, opened his mouth like he was about to say something, shook his head, and marched into the kitchen. That couldn't have been the first time Desiree had stood up to him. They certainly had a strange dynamic, those two. The mudroom door closed. Frank was gone. I wondered what, if anything, he had planned. Could he know what we were going to do?

"Danny!" Desiree raised her voice.

"What?" I asked.

"I said, we better get going," she told me. "That is, as soon as you're done spacing out." She rolled her eyes and smiled.

"Sorry," I said. "Lost in thought."

"You'll have plenty of time to think on the way," she said, placing the lunches and canteens on the counter. "I'm gonna grab a couple things in my room. Can you clear the table and do the dishes? Meet me down at the shed and we'll get out of here." She headed down the hall.

After cleaning up the kitchen, I grabbed the food and canteens for our trip and walked over to the sliding door. Acer was there, reporting for duty. And he knew the drill. The second he heard the glass slide open, he bolted down the stairs to the shed and waited, looking back like he was saying, "You're coming, Danny, right? Over here, to where the treats are? Of course you are! Well then, hurry up!"

I got to the shed and pushed on the door. There were two backpacks leaning against the wall, underneath where the mining equipment hung. They were smaller than the two Frank and I had taken. I put the bag lunches and canteens down on the wooden floor, zipped open the small front compartments on the packs, and put a bag and a canteen in each.

I grabbed the handles on the packs and lifted to test the weight. Definitely lighter than the previous loads, but still considerable. I looked inside one of them. Rope, gloves, a hoodie, and what looked like a battery-powered lantern. There was also a little metal box, about eight by three by two. I popped it open. It was a miniature tool set. I wondered why we would need that. I re-zipped the packs, grabbed a treat for the dog, and left the shed.

Acer was sitting patiently on his hind legs, eyes tracking the treat like a radar. I wanted him to earn his treat, but I couldn't tell him to sit, since he already was.

"Acer, stand up." I used my best professional animal trainer voice. His ears pricked up but he didn't move.

"Acer, roll over." Again with the ears, but nothing more.

"No, it's like this. Watch me." Desiree had appeared behind me. She wore a brown flannel shirt rolled up to her elbows, jeans, and hiking boots. A paisley-patterned purple bandana was tied around her head.

"Give me the treat," she said, holding her hand out. I did.

"Now back away." I did.

"Acer." She said the word robotically, zero emotion attached to it. Acer's ears went up. It wasn't the way you would normally talk to an animal, but I can't exactly explain how. Then she extended her empty hand toward him, flat and palm down, fingers together.

"Down," Desiree slowly and calmly commanded, lowering her hand until it was about two feet off the ground. Acer extended his front legs and lay down onto his stomach. Desiree waited for a moment. Then she tossed the treat toward the dog. He snapped it out of the air and swallowed it in the same motion.

"We have a long hike ahead of us," she said, pushing open the shed door and grabbing the two backpacks by their handles. "We should get going." Desiree handed me a pack and I slid it on. She put on the other one and closed the door to the shed, then looked at me.

"You ready?" I nodded yes, and we were off. I turned to see if Acer was coming. He wasn't. He was at the shed, lying down, his head resting between his front paws. He looked worried. Did he know something, or sense something? No, ridiculous. He was a dog. He just didn't want to go. Probably tired.

After a while, the trail narrowed a bit and the trees along each side leaned in toward us. There was plenty of room to walk side-by-side, but Desiree walked in front while I hung back a bit.

"Do you know how to get to the Witch's Nose?" I called out to her, as much to break the silence as to get an answer.

"I have a pretty good idea," Desiree called back to me, not stopping nor turning around. She pulled the straps from the backpack off her shoulders and moved it in front of her. I couldn't see what she was doing. Then, a folded piece of paper appeared in her hand. She lifted it above her head and waved it back and forth.

"What is that?" I asked.

"A drawing," she called back to me.

"How's a drawing supposed to help us get there?"

Desiree stopped. I caught up. We stood under the branches of an oak tree, the late morning sunshine sifting through its shady canopy. Tiny dots of sweat appeared through her bandana.

"Last night," she said quietly, "I snuck into Frank's room and took the map. Well, borrowed it, technically."

She handed the map to me and I examined the familiar, confusing swirl of colors. I felt my face heat up. Something in between shock, anger and fear worked its way through me.

"You stole Warrant Officer's map from Frank?" I asked, incredulous.

"Relax, Danny," she answered in her typical *don't worry about it* tone. "I didn't *steal* anything. Just borrowed it while he slept - took it to my room long enough to copy it real quick. Then returned it."

"How do you know he was asleep?" I asked her. "What if he was just pretending, and he knew what you were doing?"

"So?" she asked nonchalantly, shrugging her shoulders.

"*So*," I said, handing the map back to her, "If he knew you wanted the map, he would know *why*. He would know where we're going."

Desiree didn't respond while she folded her drawing and put it away. Warmer air had infiltrated the crisp morning and was taking hold. Either that, or my body temperature had risen with the news of Desiree's escapade into Frank's room. I reached for my water bottle and took a deep swig. She did the same.

"Well?" I asked, hoping for an explanation that I knew was coming, because she always had one. Just not usually something I would expect. What followed fit the pattern.

"Danny, I don't think Frank thinks you have the guts to pull off something like this." It wasn't the response I expected, and it hurt at first, but only because it was true. I wouldn't have done this unless Desiree had taken the lead.

"Does he think *you* have the guts for it?" I asked her.

"I'm not sure," she said. "But here's what I believe: Frank slept through my stealth mission into his room last night. He thinks you and I are out on a hike, and he's going to be at Mama's property all day, doing what he does."

"But you don't know for sure."

"No, I don't," she responded. "For all I know, he could be out here in the woods as we speak, watching us, stalking us. But that's not what my gut tells me." The forest grew quiet. In my mind's eye, I saw Frank, in full camouflage, hunched behind a tree, binoculars trained on us. Or maybe even a gun.

To Frank, I was one of the Others, the people that had showed up not too many generations ago and had ruined forever his family's traditions and culture. I was the enemy. If he were to catch me inside the sacred space of the Witch's Nose, I didn't want to imagine what he might do. All his pent-up rage, all his sadness, would find a target in me.

"But that's not what my gut tells me." OK, Desiree. I hope your gut is right.

Chapter XXIII: Closer

Have you ever been somewhere at different times, with different people, and experienced that place completely differently? That's what my experience was on the way to the Witch's Nose. With Frank, the trip was about trying to keep up, battling the changing elevations and surfaces, sweat, exhaustion, fear. With Desiree it was about appreciating the beauty surrounding us, recognizing landmarks along the way, and despite my anxiety about what we were doing, enjoying Desiree's company. A lot.

Frank and Desiree had something in common. Both could be difficult to talk to, but in different ways. Frank simply refused to speak, until he suddenly did, and what followed was unpredictable: anger, information, sarcasm, even a question on occasion. Desiree, on the other hand, was quick to start a conversation, but you had to pay attention, because her logic could be confusing. What would be an obvious thought to her might be something that I had never considered before.

The sky darkened. Out in the woods, it could happen quickly. Sometimes it was just one cloud, passing in front of the sun, and then the sky would brighten up again almost instantly. Other times, when a weather system was rolling in, the change came slowly, hard to notice unless you were tuned into it. This was one of those times.

The switchbacks had started, and Desiree was already one turn ahead, walking in the opposite direction. She smiled, a smile of excitement. Seeing joy in her face energized me. I knew I was in for a workout as we climbed the mountain, but at that moment I didn't mind.

We cleared the switchbacks and slipped between the Awkward Boulders (I had named them that and when I told Desiree, she laughed). Ahead of us lay the sloping meadow, which, despite being picturesque, was tough to climb.

"You need a rest?" Desiree asked, stopping to turn around and look back down at the switchbacks.

"I'm ok."

"Well, I do," she said.

I was secretly glad. We sat on the boulders in the shade of two cottonwood trees and ate the peanut butter and jelly sandwiches from the paper bags and drank some water.

"Do you think we'll find it?" Desiree asked.

"Find what?"

I knew exactly what she was talking about.

"You know."

She knew I knew.

"I don't know," I answered her. "I really don't."

"I do," she said, wiping peanut butter from the corner her mouth with her sleeve. "How do you feel about it?"

"I guess...nervous and excited."

"Me too."

We finished our meal, slid the packs back on, and began the trek up the sloped meadow. I managed to keep up with Desiree, who didn't seem to be struggling at all. Up ahead, the jagged

146

spires of rock that I remembered from the hike with Frank reached out toward each other, sharp granite and limestone daggers frozen in time. As we approached, Desiree turned back to me like she was saying, *"Check this out!"* We pulled our packs off before sliding between the rocks.

We entered my favorite part of the trek - the cool, shady dome of trees, the natural amphitheater that kept the heat at bay. The flat trail narrowed. Desiree stopped for a moment and looked up at the fingers of dusty light that beamed through the tall branches. I couldn't tell what she was thinking.

Next was moonscape. Moon. Part of 'moon' is an Indo-European root shared with Greek, meaning "month," and the Latin part, *metiri*, "to measure." A long time ago, people used the same blurry, oblong moon now visible overhead to measure time. I hadn't measured time since I had slipped and fallen a few days back. Days that felt like years.

On we went. The last time here, with Frank, I had marveled at the sheer drop down the mountain on the right side of the trail and imagined hearing the rumble of Bull Run River far below. This time, my brain ran a quick movie clip, starring me as a careless hiker, slipping and falling, careening down the side of the mountain, gaining speed, smashing against trees and boulders. So I focused on the left side of the trail, running my hand against the almost-vertical, rough and pockmarked rock wall. I pushed the bad movie from my mind, and switching gears, pondered instead how over the next billions of years, every inch of the gargantuan rock I was touching would slowly disintegrate into individual grains of sand.

We were moving downhill now. The trail meandered back and forth. Pretty easy on the legs, but I knew what was next: Frank's rollercoaster, which combined the zigzagging lefts and rights with thigh-burning ups and downs. I tried a different approach than last time, when I couldn't keep up and was doused with water as punishment. I hustled forward to catch up to Desiree, who had been walking ahead of me by fifteen feet or so.

I pulled even with her as the first incline began and the trail widened. She looked across at me with just a hint of a competitive smile and increased her pace enough to move ahead of me by a foot or two. I caught up. We reached the apex of one of the hills. She started running, a devious burst of laughter trailing behind her like car exhaust. I chased her.

She stopped so quickly we almost collided. In silent agreement we took off our packs and drank. I was breathing hard and could feel my heart beating double-time, more from exhilaration than exhaustion. I wasn't in any better shape than when Frank and I had traversed this part of the journey; it was Desiree. She made me forget how tired I was, energized me.

I caught my breath and looked around. Something was familiar about where we stood, but I couldn't place it. Have you ever struggled to come up with a word, like a place or a name, that you know that you know, but you can't do it? It was that right-on-the-tip-of-my-tongue feeling. Only when you stop trying to remember does it come to you. I stopped trying.

Desiree had pulled out the makeshift map she had copied from Frank's version and was holding it up against the horizon, alternating between looking at the dense forest spread out in front of us and the diagram she had drawn.

Then, I knew.

"It's there," I said, pointing. We were standing on the very spot that Frank had stopped to look at his map, where he had pointed out to me the rivers and told me the dimensions of the valley floor, the place I had first seen the Witch's Nose.

148

Her eyes followed my finger to the maverick outcropping of rock that was our destination. Its color was different than before, an incongruous bluish-steel hue. Seeing it again made it real. Thinking about going inside of it made me sick to my stomach.

We took off toward it, the Witch's Nose tracking me like the moon, silent and stealthy, until it finally ducked and hid behind the same grove of pines I remembered from Frank's hike. The trail we were on disappeared, leaving me again following Desiree, the sound of crunching leaves and sticks underfoot.

The seriousness of where we were going, of what we might find, generated a weight, a pressure, that pushed down on my body. The last time I walked here, I had nearly collapsed from sheer exhaustion. Now, I was fine physically, but felt trapped in apprehension.

Desiree's methodical strides gave no hint as to how she was feeling; was she experiencing the same tension? I suppose I could have asked her, but I didn't want her to know how I felt. Although, as we continued walking and she looked back at me, I sensed she knew how I felt, and understood.

We were at the base of the rock. I didn't remember anything about this section of the trail, the final leg of the trek, up to the opening. I remember being completely exhausted, the edge of the backpack frame digging into my back, Frank dousing me with water. Everything else was a blur.

The trail wasn't remarkable, considering what it led to. It was kind of like walking up the seams of a giant baseball, curving around and up at the same time, feeling the gain in elevation because my legs were burning, forgetting about my anxiety because I was trying to keep up with Desiree, because if I couldn't, maybe she would think I was a loser.

Bent over, hands on knees, breathing heavily. We had made it. Desiree pulled off her pack and walked over to me. She didn't look tired; quite the opposite, in fact. The last vertical push up to the Witch's Nose seemed to have reinvigorated her. She reached out her hand.

"Gimme five," she said. "We made it." I stood up and made an awkward attempt to meet her palm with mine, but she pulled it away.

"Too slow!" she laughed. "Let's rest up a bit," she said. "It's going to get dark soon, but if Frank's father described the tunnels accurately, it won't matter if it's light up here on the surface or not."

I put my pack down on Frank's rock ledge and turned around. Desiree was leaning against the smooth, almost too-perfect nose, her back and head pushed up against it. Her eyes were closed. I didn't know if she was resting or meditating. I turned back the other way and stepped up on the rock ledge. It was that time in the late afternoon when the sunlight changed the color of the forest quickly, each green a different hue, a new saturation, the light familiar for a second, then new again.

I stepped back down. The almost square outline of the ashes from Frank's fire were still there, under my foot. I was surprised the wind hadn't taken them. I bent down and pinched some, rubbing them between my index finger and thumb. I opened my hand and the ashes caught a gentle updraft and rose, twisting and chasing each other, until I could no longer see them against the gray of the rock. *Who do you think you're more like, Danny? The Original People, or the Others?*

"Hey, come here."

I walked over to her. She was still leaning back against the rock, the sweat-soaked bandana resting around her neck. Her brow was furrowed, like she was pondering one of life's great mysteries.

"What angle do you think this nose is?" It was definitely the first time in my life I had been asked that.

"Maybe about forty-five degrees?" I guessed. "The rock's almost bisecting a ninety-degree angle, between vertical and horizontal."

"Wow, someone knows his math," she said. "But does he also know his noses? Here's another question: if this was an actual, functioning, massive human nose, what would the average size of one of the boogers be?"

"Given the width of the nostrils," I answered, sounding as academic as possible, "I would calculate a typical booger from this nose would have a circumference of about three and a half feet." Desiree lifted her back off of the rock and looked at me with her head tilted to the side, like she was sizing me up.

"Seriously?" she asked me. And with that question, I had finally gotten her back.

"No."

"You got me!" she giggled, bringing her hands up to her temples. "We're even now."

"No, we're not," I replied, smiling at her. "Not even close." She nodded in agreement and pushed herself off of the rock. We ate our sandwiches and emptied out the packs.

151

"What's with the rope?" I asked Desiree, pulling the thick cord out of my pack.

"Mm-nn-shh r-ope eel hol-ush." She had stuffed half of the sandwich into her mouth and trying to talk with it there was causing some of it to come back out, making her laugh.

"I can't understand you with your mouth full," I said.

"My mouf ithn't fool!" She chewed for a minute and then took a swig of water. "I said, I'm not sure that the rope will hold us, the original rope."

"The way Warrant Officer described it, it seems pretty sturdy," I replied.

"It may have been, but that was a long time ago," she responded. "The elements may have weakened it. But there's only one way to find out." Desiree stood and began to put the packs back together.

"Wait, we're going now?" A tiny bit of my earlier anxiety had crept into my voice.

"Can you think of a better time?" she asked. I couldn't. We slid our packs back on and made our way to the other side of the rock. The late-afternoon sun seemed to hover above the entrance to the tunnels, like light about to be captured by a black hole.

"Try the ladder," Desiree instructed. "Just give it a push down with your foot."

I tested the rope ladder with my weight leaning outward, so if I fell, I would fall forward, away from the hole. It felt absolutely solid. The ancient but effective technology of tightly wound plant fibers, combined with time, had created a robust and dependable method for entering and (hopefully) exiting the caves. We wouldn't need the rope we brought, at least not now. "I think we're good," I reported to Desiree.

"So, you ready to do this?" she asked.

"Let's do it."

My answer was full of false confidence. I wasn't ready. I was sure this was a place that I was never meant to enter, and that those who had spent time here, the Original People, had never intended for someone like me to enter. But I was also sure that the girl I was with made me feel good, and I was willing to do whatever it took to keep spending time with her. Even this.

Chapter XXIV: Into the Dark

"I'll go down first," Desiree said. "Wait until I'm on the ground down there before you start. We don't want to put any unnecessary weight on the rope." She placed a tentative foot on the top rung of the rope ladder, tested it, and then descended quickly, not looking down at where she was going, but rather, up at me, until her head disappeared beneath the rock's gray surface. I moved forward and looked down.

Desiree was on her knees, holding the battery powered lantern she had taken out of her backpack. Even with it right next to her, and some light still filtering down into the entrance, I could hardly see the dark and hazy outline of her body. Didn't bode well for our ability to navigate the caves. Maybe both lanterns combined would provide better illumination.

"There's a jump from the bottom rung down to the floor here," she yelled up to me, her words carrying a faint, hollow echo. "Come on down!"

My turn. I tightened the straps on my pack and took one more look around the surface of the Witch's Nose. I wasn't sure when, or if, I would see it again. Then I turned my back toward the hole and stepped down onto the first rung of the ladder. As I descended, I was half expecting Desiree to say something like, "Hurry up, slowpoke!" or "My grandma is faster than you!" But she said nothing, and I heard nothing. Maybe she knew I needed to concentrate on my footing, who knows. I reached the bottom rung of the rope, jumped, and landed on both feet.

We stood silently at the bottom of the entrance to the tunnels, in the dim funnel of light that the last rays of evening sun had left for us. The walls of the cavern were about ten feet apart.

It was warm and humid. I switched on my lantern. Nothing happened. I hit it once with my hand. It flickered and came on. The walls matched Warrant Officer's description: swirling brown and rust colors.

"Neither of us have ever been down here, Danny, but you read the letter," she said, looking up at the opening to the rock. Then she looked at me. "Lead the way."

"Down here," I said with as much confidence as I could muster, gesturing to our left with the lantern. It was the direction that I imagined Warrant Officer thinking his village was located, a village that this many years later must look much different, if it were there at all.

We walked, me in front. It was a shockingly quick few steps until the last trace of light disappeared behind us and we had to rely on the lanterns. I turned around to see Desiree, her lantern dark and eyes closed, left arm extended, hand following the contours of the wall. She was experiencing the caves like Frank's father had done years before, perceiving the cave not visually but through her tactile sense.

The passage alternated between about eight and fifteen feet across and maybe ten feet in height. The ground was relatively flat and made a fine crunching sound under my feet. I stopped and bent down to scoop up with my hand what I thought was going to be dirt. It wasn't. It was sharper, more granular, and black, as black as the cave walls and ceiling. It felt like shattered glass.

"Cool, huh?" Desiree had clicked back on her light and caught up to me. "It's from the ceiling. I assume you don't know much about lava tubes."

"No, I have to admit I don't."

"Let's stop where we are, sit down, take a drink, and rest your lantern batts for a bit," she suggested. "I can catch you up." My canteen was much lighter now, maybe half full. Desiree rolled up her sleeves and used the bandana to pat the sweat beads off of her forehead. Then we sat, and for the first time, I experienced total darkness.

It was the black that Warrant Officer had described. Reading about it, imagining it, was not even close to experiencing it. The dark was a something, a thick and dull and ominous something. And it was a nothing, the total absence of light and sight. I didn't know if my eyes were open or closed. It didn't matter.

"Amazing, isn't it?" Desiree asked. Her words seem to travel directly from her mouth into my ears.

"Yes."

Then I felt my hand being touched.

Her touch was so gentle, so imperceptible, that I wasn't sure it had actually happened. I had no sense of time passing. Maybe it wasn't. Maybe it had stopped.

What did it mean? *It'll be ok, Danny.* Or, *I'm glad you're here with me.* Or, *I like you.* Or maybe something else entirely. Or maybe nothing at all.

"We're sitting underneath a volcano." Hell of a way to snap me out of wherever my brain had been. "I'm not an expert - "

"- but, let me guess," I interrupted. "You've read about it." I couldn't see her face but I imagined she was smiling. "I know a little," she answered demurely.

I wasn't just hearing her voice- I was physically *sensing* it - letters and words that existed in the physical plane, traveling from her mouth into my ears. It was as if, in response to the lack of visual stimuli, my brain had reconfigured itself and was processing information in a new format.

"Sometime in the distant past, not that far away from here, there was a volcanic eruption." I saw the massive explosion in my mind's eye.

"When volcanoes erupt, some of the lava is pushed with great force underground and burns its way through anything it encounters. The lava can create many subterranean channels, like tentacles, that emanate from the eruption point, and some that stem off of other channels. The area around the channels cools pretty quick, but the channels themselves stay hot for a long time.

"Finally the lava cools, dries, and collapses, leaving tubes like the one we're in. Imagine some alien glove with a hundred massive fingers," she said. "I guess you could say we're inside one of the fingers." I liked Desiree's analogies. They were weird, but I got them.

"A lot of these lava tubes are close to the surface," she continued. "When a tube can no longer support whatever is above it, it will collapse. Sometimes it's only partial; in that case, we would see what they call a skylight - a break in the top of the tube."

"It would be great if we could find some of these skylights," I said. "It would give us light, and maybe a way out."

"Maybe," Desiree responded, "but they're also dangerous places. Skylights are extremely unstable, as are the areas around them. We could easily cause a further collapse and become trapped. Then we'd die, and we'd be having a bad day."

"That would definitely qualify as a bad day," I agreed.

"But," she said, "there *may* be a skylight stable enough, solid enough, to allow us to access the outside. Of course, the third possibility is that we don't find any at all."

"And in that case?" I asked. I knew she'd have a response. She always did.

"In that case, we need to backtrack to the original opening. Remember Hansel and Gretel?"

"Is this a trick question?" I asked.

"No," she said. "Not everybody does."

"Yep," I told her. "They were the kids who were sent into the woods and found their way back home by laying a trail of breadcrumbs."

"Well, I wanted something that *we* could put down to mark our route, in case we needed to find our way back. I thought about thermoluminescent rocks - that would have been great. But I had no time to come up with anything." I wasn't sure what thermoluminescent rocks were and didn't ask.

"What will we use?"

"Nothing," Desiree replied, clicking her light back on. It produced a weak, alien yellow-green color that rested unnaturally on the cave walls. Then she pulled out something from her pants pocket. As she held it to the light, it became a folded piece of paper and a charcoal pencil.

"I'll sketch the way," she said, unfolding the paper. It was blank and folded into squares, each about a square inch. "We can use a grid system," she said. "Hold this out." I took the top and bottom of the paper and oriented it landscape-style, then pulled it taut. She placed the tip of the pencil on a square in the middle of what was my right edge of the paper.

"We entered here," Desiree explained, making a thick 'x' with the charcoal. "We walked down this passage (here she traced through three squares a line that pointed to the other side of the page) to about - here."

"How do we know how many squares we've traveled?" I asked her.

"We don't," she said. "I figure that, at an average pace, I would mark through one square every ten minutes."

I had questions, like, *how are going to keep track of time without a watch?* But the answers would have no effect on what we were doing down here. She folded up the map and stuck the charcoal pencil in her front shirt pocket.

"How do you feel?" The question caught me off guard.

"Nervous and excited."

But there was another feeling there as well, one I couldn't quite assign a word to. While Desiree had been explaining lava tube formation and grid patterns, part of my mind had wandered. I was remembering the conversation Desiree and I had back in her bedroom, when she had asked me if I believed Warrant Officer's story. I had told her yes.

And I still believed it. Which was scary to me, because there was a chance we might actually discover what we were looking for. Which meant we might run into the people that Warrant Officer saw and interacted with. Which made me feel nervous and excited. But something else as well, something I couldn't put a finger on.

"We should get moving," Desiree said, standing up and stretching. I stood as well. "We'll be good with just one lantern for now."

We started off again, my lantern's light performing an eerie dance along the contours of the walls, reflecting off of smooth horizontal swirls that enveloped jagged, geometric protrusions. The ground was flat and smooth. It was like people long ago had spent significant time clearing the path; for what purpose, I couldn't imagine. We stopped. Desiree unfolded the paper, pulled out the pencil and marked a square. We moved on. It got warmer. It felt like we were descending.

"Cool thing about these places," Desiree said, switching into tour guide mode again, "is that conditions down here are dry and arid enough so that if people left things down here, they would still be in good shape even after thousands of years, provided they weren't disturbed and there were no skylight collapses."

"Like the little three-legged bowls, right?" I asked her.

No answer.

"Like the bowls?"

I knew that Desiree sometimes "checked out" of our conversations. I didn't take it personally; I figured that since her brain worked so hard most of the time, it needed an occasional pit stop. She stopped walking, pulled out the grid paper and charcoal, and made a mark. She had made five or six of them in total. Despite being a first-hand witness to her mapping progress, I had no idea where we were.

We came to a spot in the tunnel where a wall divided it into two parallel passages, possibly the same area that Warrant Officer referred to; I couldn't be sure. We took the left-hand side of the split.

Having compared Warrant Officer's description of his time in the tubes to what I am writing here, one thing is clear: Franklin Summers is far and away a better writer than I am. His recall and descriptions of the journey through the tunnels was like reading an adventure novel. I felt like I was right there with him. Even under the pressure of reading it out loud to Frank, it was riveting, compelling. Mine isn't. But it's the best I can do. I hope it's good enough.

We walked down the left-hand tunnel. And another tunnel. And another. So many charcoal-filled squares that I lost count. And I really didn't care how many, because each one was another ten minutes of time I got to spend with Desiree. But still, that weird feeling.

Then, for no discernable reason, we stopped and sat. We turned off the lantern and just listened to the darkness. I took a deep breath and realized that my unknown uncomfortable feeling was gone. It was just us. Was there anything else except us, except here, except now?

Yes.

There was a light.

I stood.

It was a glow so faint that I couldn't tell if it was real.

I tapped Desiree on the shoulder.

She looked up at me and clicked the lantern on.

I pointed. She turned the lantern off, stood and looked.

I don't know what was going through her mind at that exact moment. But I clearly remember exactly what I was thinking. It was two words:

Holy crap.

I was having an out-of-body experience, floating behind myself and Desiree, watching the two of us move down the passage, the glow getting brighter until it filled every crack and crevice in the lava tube. It was above us.

It was...a *skylight*.

Of course. What was I thinking it could be? Stupid, Danny. Grow up. Get real. It was the result of a tunnel collapse. Grayish-red and brown boulders had tumbling down upon each other, leaving a huge gash open to the surface. But it was night time. What was the light?

I lifted myself up onto one of the smaller rocks, then continued climbing, reaching for footholds and testing the stability of different ledges, until my head drew even with the top of the ground, and I was able to view the source of the light.

It was the moon.

"What's going on up there?" Desiree asked.

"It's the moon," I responded.

I looked around. The area was covered with a thick layer of fallen leaves. The big rock was no longer visible, so we must have traveled a considerable distance underground. But the trees and other vegetation in the area offered no clues as to our location, and there were no other recognizable landmarks. So, in other words, I had no idea where we were.

"Can you tell where we are?" she asked.

"No idea," I answered. I assumed she would be coming up through the skylight to check out the area for herself, since her mapping and orientating skills were superior to mine. I was wrong.

"Come back down," she told me.

I reversed course and carefully made my way back down. We stood, bathed in clean, white moonlight, next to one of the big rocks. Desiree leaned her weight against it, holding the folded grid paper between her thumb and index finger.

"Well Danny, we have two choices," she said. "We can get out of here right now. It won't take long for us to figure out where we are and make our way back to Mama's."

"The safe choice," I said. "The logical choice."

"Yes, safe and logical," she continued. "Don't get me wrong, it's been awesome exploring the tube system. But, besides the entrance, this may be the only way out. There's no way of knowing. And if we keep going, there's no guarantee we will be able to find our way back to the entrance, or back to the sky-light."

"We could be trapped in here," I added. "And we have minimal food, water, and battery power left."

"Seems like we've made our decision," she said, exhaling and looking up through the skylight.

"Seems like it," I echoed.

"Keep going?" she asked.

"Absolutely."

It didn't make sense. It wasn't logical. It wasn't the safe choice. But we both knew that we had to continue looking, and we knew that the other person felt the same way.

The tubes turned one way and then the other, rose and fell and sometimes split into two or three separate tubes. We would choose one by looking at each other and deciding. After a few more ten-minute stops, Desiree quit filling in the grid squares. I guess I should have been concerned that the only system we had to at least try to keep track of where we had been was now folded into my companion's pocket, but I didn't care.

Everything looked the same. I couldn't tell if we had been through a particular tunnel before. We were low on water and out of food. My throat hurt. Maybe it was from inhaling the tiny silicate particles we must have been kicking up from the tunnel floor. I stopped thinking. One foot down. Then another. Repeat. We were two-legged blind rats in a black, unending maze.

"Danny."

Just two syllables. She had said them a hundred times since I met her. But something in the way she said my name, this time.

No.

"Danny." *No, it's not real.*

I kept my eyes closed. Because if I opened them, I might see something I wouldn't understand, something that might change me.

Black
/blak/

Adjective

Of the very darkest color owing to the absence of or complete absorption of light.

"I lied when you asked me how I felt," I said.

"You did?"

"Yes," I answered. "When you asked me how I was feeling, I told you I was nervous and excited. But I lied."

"So how do you feel?"

"Scared."

"Me too," she said. "Let's be scared together. Take my hand."

I did. My eyes were wide open.

Chapter XXV: The Source

The glow came from the right side of the tunnel on the left, just like Warrant Officer had described, and grew stronger as we approached. I read somewhere that a déjà vu is simply the brain replaying something a millisecond after it happens in real life, so that it seems like a memory. How can I describe a light that was totally alien to me and yet, completely familiar? This was the strongest deja vu I had ever experienced. I knew, *knew*, this was the first time I had been here and done this; but a memory existed nonetheless - a real memory. I know, it doesn't make sense.

I was overcome with an overwhelming sense of serenity and peace. My thoughts stopped racing. My breathing slowed, regulated by some inner metronome I did not know existed. It was like the Source was saying to me, "Danny, I know this is new and scary, but everything is going to be all right. There is nothing that you have to do, nothing to worry about." I turned to look at Desiree. She was pure tranquility and joy. The reflection of the glow flickered in her eyes. I felt immensely happy I was with her and that we were there.

Maybe you've seen a video of the sun when a filter has been applied to it that allows the viewer to glimpse its surface, the chaotic swirling movement of immensely powerful magnetic currents. That's as close as I can get to sharing with you, with written words, what the Source looked like. No word I am aware of can precisely relate to you how it hovered above the basin that was built into the wall of the lava tube. *Perched* is too fixed of a term. *Suspended* is about right.

We sat.

We waited.

Nothing happened.

Maybe our holding hands would the spark to begin whatever was going to happen.

It wasn't.

"Didn't Warrant Officer mention something about some broken pottery that was here?"

"Yes, he did." There was nothing on the ground in front of us except some small rocks and the omnipresent fine volcanic powder.

"Aren't some ancient people supposed to... materialize?" she asked me. "Isn't that what happened when Warrant Officer was here?"

"Yes, that's what he said," I told her. "I don't know why they aren't. Let's just stay here for a while and watch."

We sat cross-legged, holding hands. My mind bounced between the insane reality that we had found the Source, and the effervescent feeling coursing through my body caused by the fact that I was holding hands with Desiree. By now, she knew the hand-holding didn't have an effect on the Source, so the only other explanation was that she wanted to hold my hand.

"Something's happening."

Imagine an equation. The exact variables don't matter. Neither do the coefficients, nor the constants. You are as familiar with this equation as anything you've ever known. You've always known it; it's a part of you, of your genetic code, your DNA. See the equation floating in front of you, in three dimensions. Reach your right hand toward it, fingers outstretched, and it responds, turning away from you, rotating along its y-axis. Pull your hand back and the equation rotates toward you. Your left hand controls the spin on its x-axis, like a locomotive on a train roundhouse. Put your palms together as close as they can be without touching, thumbs facing up. Now touch your fingers together, barely, imperceptibly. Watch as the equation zooms in toward you, closer, closer, until it blots out your vision completely and fills the room and you - you yourself! - hover on the surface of one of the terms; now look down, touch it, know that the term is made up of, created from, the equation itself, and the equation is built again from more terms, variables, coefficients, building blocks made from smaller and smaller perfect copies. Keep pulling your hands apart and you are now *inside* the equation, riding an infinite fractal deeper and deeper into -

"What the hell are you doing?"

Justin, at some point in your life you have probably tripped or run into something accidentally and it hurts. And your first thought is, *I hope no one saw that. This is really embarrassing.* When Desiree asked me what I was doing, that was my first reaction. I felt like I had made a mistake. Looking back, I think it was because I didn't know if was actually doing those things I just described to you, the manipulating of the equation, or if I had been imagining it and, in reality, had been sitting there doing something weird, like, I don't know, moaning and waving my hands in the air for no reason and looking like an idiot while Desiree watched.

"I don't know," I answered. "What did you see?"

"Something...wonderful." She was smiling, and the shimmering golden glow of the Source made her more beautiful than I had ever seen her.

"You were manipulating...controlling... these free-floating, glittering numbers and letters, long streams of them, all with

168

your hands and fingers. I can't describe what exactly, or how. What did you think you were doing?"

"I thought I - I don't know, I thought I was having a weird dream, or watching someone else - "

The Source was changing, re-forming. It was rectangular now, the longer sides on the top and bottom, about the size of large PC screen. The rate of gyration and twisting had increased. Within the movement, two shapes were forming, dark smudges parallel to each other in the middle of the display. They became human-shaped, blurry heads, sticks for arms and legs, one person bent at the waist, leaning forward; the other, much larger, sitting cross-legged, and watching. The resolution sharpened. The scene became less ethereal, more real. The bent-forward body was a girl; the bigger one, sitting and observing, a boy. They were under the Witch's Nose, in a lava tube, our lava tube, exactly where Desiree and I sat right now. Next to them sat a cube-shaped tin box with picture of a clown on it and a red-tipped handle attached.

Then I knew something more, something that I couldn't have known. And I felt sick.

"I know them," I said.

"What do you mean?" Desiree asked.

"I know them - who they are," I stammered. "Linda, the girl, is my mother. The boy's name is Davis. They were friends growing up. Davis is the man that showed up at my house after I fell. And I now know what he was looking for."

What we witnessed next was like a screenplay, like one written for a television show. I have taken the liberty of writing it that way, because that's the way it felt at the time.

169

Chapter XXVI: Linda and Davis

FADE IN

INT- LAVA TUBE - NIGHT

DAVIS
Linda, I don't think this is smart.

LINDA looks at DAVIS, tilts her head to the side, mocks him with a deep, dumb-sounding voice.

LINDA
Linda, I don't think this is smart.

DAVIS averts his eyes. His body slumps.

LINDA (CONT'D.)
Davis, *thinking* isn't exactly your strong suit. Please just shut your mouth and let me figure this out. Now if I can somehow just pull off a piece - a section, or whatever, of this - stuff…

LINDA tries in vain to take hold of the SOURCE while it dances in and out of her hands. Twice she grabs hold of it and almost secures it before it slips from her grasp, seemingly taunting her.

DAVIS
Need help?

LINDA
Do I *look* like I need help? Just hold the damn box Davis, and when I put the stuff in there, close it up real tight. Do you think you can handle that?

                                    DAVIS
What about the clown?

                                    LINDA
What clown?

                                    DAVIS
The clown in the jack-in-the-box.

LINDA stops what she's doing and glares at DAVIS.

                                    LINDA
Seriously? You think I'd leave the stupid jack-in-the-box
clown inside the box?

                                    DAVIS
I didn't know.

                                    LINDA
No, you didn't. You don't know much. Dammit, this stuff
cannot be grabbed! There's nothing here to hold on to!

LINDA continues to struggle to take some of the SOURCE.
The SOURCE continues to gyrate between her fingers and in
and out of her hands.

                                    DAVIS
Here, let me try.

                                    LINDA
Oh, that's a great idea. What could you possibly do that I
can't?

                                    DAVIS
Just let me.

                                    171

LINDA

I can't believe I'm doing this.

LINDA moves over. DAVIS takes her place in front of the SOURCE.

LINDA (CONT'D.)

Here. Give me the box to hold. In the extremely unlikely event you're successful, put the stuff in here.

DAVIS

OK.

DAVIS crosses his legs, takes a deep, relaxing breath, and closes his eyes. LINDA is annoyed.

LINDA

Why are your eyes closed?

DAVIS

I have an idea. Close your eyes, too.

LINDA

I'm not closing my eyes. This is the epitome of stupid.

DAVIS

The what?

LINDA is approaching her boiling point. She yells at DAVIS.

LINDA

You are a moron!

DAVIS

Just close your eyes for a second. Please.

                    LINDA

This is such a massive waste of my time. OK, they're
closed. Now what?

                    DAVIS

Imagine that some of this golden stuff is going into the box.

                    LINDA

What? This was your great idea? To *imagine*?

                    DAVIS

Just see the stuff going into the box in your mind. Let's be
quiet.

                    LINDA

This is crazy. OK.

                    DAVIS

There. Open your eyes.

LINDA keeps her eyes closed.

                    LINDA

There? There what?

                    DAVIS

Check the tin.

LINDA peers into the tin box, a shocked look appearing on
her face.

                    LINDA

Oh my God. This can't be happening. But I see it with my
own eyes. We did it!

DAVIS

You have to be calm, you have to be nice. You have to see it happen. Put the top on it.

LINDA gets onto her knees. She uses her body weight to push the flat, metal top down onto the container. It pops closed. They stand.

LINDA

I'll hold it. Let's go.

DAVIS

But we'll share it, right Linda?

LINDA

Of course, we'll share it. I just want to take it to my place first, check it out. You know, make some initial, uh...observations and measurements.

DAVIS

OK, I trust you.

LINDA

Of course you do. Why wouldn't you? Let's get out of here.

Chapter XXVII: The Knife

The Source had settled back into its portal again, its glow considerably less strong than it had been, like it was recharging, regenerating, after having expended energy on us. Desiree and I looked at each other, a look that I'm sure no two humans had ever exchanged. I was drained. We drank the rest of our water.

"Were you watching what I was watching?" Desiree asked me, astonished.

"Yes."

"OK, just checking," she replied. "When were your mom and that guy, Davis, down here?"

"Jeez, had to be at least 30 years ago."

"Your mom's kind of a b…"

"Yeah," I interrupted, finishing the word in my mind. "I guess she was, at least when she was a kid."

"So, does your mom still have some of the stuff?" Desiree asked me, her words not hiding disdain.

"I don't know. I guess she might. If she didn't, I don't see why Davis would come looking for it."

"I brought something." She tossed it to me. It was a Rubik's Cube. I had seen one before, but never held one. It looked and felt new. Each of its six sides was a mixed-up combination of red, green, blue, white, yellow, and orange.

"Why did you bring this?" I asked her.

"I don't know," she said. "I thought it might work. As a containment vessel."

"What do we do?"

"Let's try what seemed to work for Linda and Davis. If it doesn't, we'll try something else. Hold the cube out like this." She turned her palm up and extended her hand like she was presenting it as an offering. I put the cube on my hand and reached out toward the Source.

"Ok, now we close our eyes and imagine that- what did Davis say? - 'see the stuff going in'."

Desiree's eyes were already closed. I closed mine and pictured a thin stream of material flowing from the Source directly into the Rubik's Cube, finding the spaces between the sides and edges and sliding its way down into the center.

"Are your eyes still closed?" she asked.

"Yes," I said.

"Did you visualize it?"

"Yes."

"OK," she said. "When I count to three, open your eyes. One. Two. Three. Open."

Nothing had happened. The cube sat on my upturned palm, motionless. Nothing about the Source appeared to be different either.

"I think we need to clear our minds for it to work," Desiree suggested. "We can't have a bunch of other thoughts zooming around in our brains." Considering all that had happened and where we were at the moment, trying not to think about anything was difficult, but I took a few deep breaths and tried to imagine what zero activity in my brain would look and feel like. Just nothing. An empty, hollow space.

"You ready?" Desiree asked.

"Yes."

"Now visualize."

I didn't visualize anything. Or maybe I visualized nothing. I just focused on keeping my mind clear, empty and hollow. Breathe. Empty and hollow. Breathe.

"Open your eyes," she said. "Let's take a look." The cube was still in my hand. But it was *solved*. It was solved! I turned it over in my hands. Each of the Rubik's Cube's six sides was a solid color.

"Wow!" Desiree blurted, laughing out loud. "Did you feel it move?"

"No, nothing!" I gasped. "So freaky."

"Let me see it," she said.

I handed it to her and she brought it up close to her face at eye level. "It's in there," she said. "The Source. I can see the glow. I can *feel* it. Like a vibration."

She rotated the front side one turn to the right. It snapped back to its original position almost too fast to perceive. She smiled at me. She turned the top side, then the left side, then the right. The cube instantly solved itself, undoing the three turns so rapidly that the movement was difficult to see.

"We did it," she said.

"Yes, we did."

Then what I didn't want to ask her came falling out of my mouth. "Are you sure you want to take it out of here?"

"Danny," she said, tilting her head to the side, "don't start that again. We're *taking* it. Think about it: if it didn't *want* to be taken, we couldn't have captured some of it." I wasn't convinced of her logic. Desiree was assuming that the Source was actually aware of what was going on, that it could make decisions - that it could *think*. It was too much to wrap my tired brain around.

"There will be plenty of time to figure out what this stuff really does, and maybe even what it is," Desiree said. "But we should get going. It's gotta be morning soon. The skylight will be easier to find."

We stood. I put on my backpack. She clicked on her lantern and put the Rubik's Cube inside of a small pocket in the top of her pack, zipped it, and put the straps over her shoulders.

"Shall we?"

We were walking again. The last few days I had been laser-focused on finding this amazing stuff. Now that we had found it, and had taken some of it with us, I should have been incredibly excited. And I was - kind of. But knowing that my mother had been down here, and that she had lied to me about not knowing who the man in the house was and what he had been looking for, felt like a weight tied to me. But despite all that, I was with a girl I really liked. It was a new feeling, a great feeling, and I didn't want it to end.

"I see it," Desiree said, looking back at me. I did, too. Fifty yards away, clean morning sunlight streaming down into the tube. We had reached the skylight. We scaled the rocks and then we were filling our lungs with fresh, cool mountain air again.

"We did it." The flat tone of her voice didn't match our accomplishment. Something wasn't right. She took off her backpack and pulled out the cube. "This is yours," she said, handing it to me.

"You want me to carry it on our way back to Mama's?"

Desiree didn't respond. She turned and walked away from me, maybe ten feet, in the direction of a small evergreen that was painted in a thick coat of dark green moss and covered with dew. Fog obscured anything beyond her, and in the morning light her body looked like it could have been part of the tree's branch structure, part of the forest.

"Danny, you haven't thought this all the way through," she said. "Frank's whole life is centered around finding a connection between him and Warrant Officer. The stuff we have with us is the closest he'll ever get to that connection. Frank knows where we went. He knows what we were trying to find. I can't show up at Mama's with this stuff."

"Ok, so we bury it," I suggested. "Like Frank buried the letters. It's a big forest out here. We can find a place, there's no problem as far as that goes."

"No," Desiree said. "*You* have to take it. Think about it, Danny - it was all about *you* down there. The equation, the numbers...even the people. All of it." She walked a few feet farther away, almost disappearing into the green.

"I was watching what you did," she continued, "but it made no sense to me. I was an observer. An outsider. But those numbers, they have *meaning* to you. You may not know exactly what yet, but you will." What Desiree said was true. The equation I was shown was stuck in my head. It was a part of me now. How, I wasn't sure, but it was.

"And the scene with your mom and Davis. It answers questions, important questions, that you had. The Source focused on you, Danny. You. Not me."

"Ok," I replied, "So let's say I take it with me - then what?"

"I'm going back to Mama's," she said. "My parents are coming to get me. Tomorrow will mark exactly six months at Mama's. Six months. That's how long my parents and I agreed I'd be there. It won't be easy at home. I'm not sure anything has really changed, but I'm going to try and make it work."

The tip of the knife is so sharp that you're not even aware it has broken your skin. The fine edge burrows into the subcutaneous layers of your chest and probes for a soft entrance between two ribs, piercing and filleting the soft tissue of your heart's right ventricle, the serrated side of the knife simultaneously lacerating the pulmonary valve. It is quick. It is painful. It is bloody. It is deadly.

"But how will I see you? I don't want to lose you." The words were desperate. I was desperate.

"You won't lose me," Desiree said, smiling again. "I will find you, Danny, I promise."

Epilogue

So, that's it. I found my way home. My mom and I never spoke about Davis or about the Source - what you know as C-Metal. And of course, Desiree, your mother, did find me. We found each other.

Frank followed in Warrant Officer's footsteps and joined the army. It was the closest he could get to his father. He was tailor-made for the structure the military provided and was very successful there. After his military career, he became a police officer in a town near Bent Valley.

Justin, I am reluctant to tell you more, because, in case Frank catches up to you, he can't make you tell you something you don't know. I have much more to share with you when we are together again as a family.

This bears repeating: It's a regular Rubik's Cube. Plastic. Eight corner pieces. Twelve middle edges. Six center squares.

1. Don't lose the cube. Either keep it with you or in a place no one knows about.

2. Only handle the cube when necessary. Don't turn the cube, and don't take it apart. C-Metal isn't dangerous; you just need to be ready to handle it, and right now, you're not. Not yet.

3. I know this will sound strange, but try not to think about the cube too much. In time, you'll become more familiar with the material inside of it, and you will understand.

Destroy this thumb drive.

CPSIA information can be obtained
at www.ICGtesting.com
Printed in the USA
LVHW050837110219
607105LV00006B/437/P